SEVEN FOR A SECRET NEVER TO BE TOLD

A RESORTING TO MURDER MYSTERY

DEREK D WHEELESS

While Wentworth Mansion, Peninsula Grill, Halls Chophouse, and several other locations around historic Charleston are real places you can visit, and it is recommended you do, this story is a work of fiction. Names, characters, organizations, events, and incidents are products of the author's imagination or are used fictitiously. Any resemblance to actual persons, living or dead, or actual events is coincidental.

Published by Invisible Think Books

ISBN 979-8-9859335-3-6

Cover Design: Maria Novillo Saravia at www.Beautebook.com

Editing: Barb Goffman, Jimmy Callaway, and Nathan Bransford

To Tiffany

AUTHOR'S NOTE

While Wentworth Mansion, Peninsula Grill, Halls Chophouse, and several other locations around historic Charleston are real places you can visit, and I encourage you to do so, this story is a work of fiction. Names, characters, organizations, events, and incidents are products of my imagination or are used fictitiously. Any resemblance to actual persons, living or dead, or actual events is coincidental.

DDW

If you want to keep a secret, you must also hide it from yourself.

— GEORGE ORWELL

1

———

"I'm going to murder someone in this beautiful Gothic mansion," Jaxson said, "and I need you to help me solve it."

Holiday turned an uneasy head toward her husband. He was smiling, small lines crinkling in the corners of his striking blue eyes. His midnight black hair was trimmed neatly beneath his brown leather fedora, and the collar of his matching raincoat turned up against his neck. Charleston could get chilly in October.

She leveled wide, uncertain eyes on him as his words hung in the frigid air. Did he know? Only two people had known the truth about the night Bobby died. One had promised to take the secret with her to the grave. The other was already there.

She let out a long breath and watched it transform into white steam in the cool air. "Is that the opening to your next book, dear?"

Jaxson shook his head. "It is a plea for your assistance in setting our next story in this glorious old inn! And, I don't mind saying, if my fate is to one day be murdered, this is exactly the kind of place I want it to happen."

"I love your enthusiasm for writing. I love you in your fedora." She patted his rosy cheek. "And I love you all scruffy like this. But please don't go dying on me just yet, here or anywhere. I'm not quite ready to be a widow at forty-two. We've only been married half a year."

As they stood at the bottom of the bifurcated stone staircase leading up to the front doors of downtown Charleston's historic Wentworth Mansion, she regarded the imposing red brick house, well-known for its alternating long and short white quoin corners and its recognizable charcoal, gray-tiled mansard roof. There was a gorgeous white cupola up there, too, but she couldn't see it from where they stood. Built for a wealthy 19th-century family, the house had become a boutique hotel. So many people in the last one hundred and forty years had taken those steps, entered the old inn, and stayed in its rooms. The stories the mansion could tell.

Holiday shuddered and snugged the lapels of her sandpiper-colored overcoat around her maroon scarf a little tighter.

She had told herself she would never return to the place where it had happened, where Bobby had been killed, and yet she had—two decades to the day of his murder. There had been no other way. She had to know what Daily knew. Would Daily reveal the truth about her, that Holiday had been with Bobby the night he'd been murdered, that she'd been an accomplice in his death? Holiday had formulated a plan. She would go back to the house one more time. She would find out what Daily knew and deny it. And then she'd bury the truth so her new husband would never know. And she'd use him to do it.

Holiday stiffened in the shadows cast by the house

silhouetted against the lowering afternoon sun. Did Wentworth hide the secrets it knew?

Of course, she'd have to get past Jaxson's suspicions to do what needed to be done. She'd asked him to divert his return trip to Dallas from a writing conference, and he'd agreed, meeting her in Charleston instead. He'd peppered her with questions in the cab from CHS about what was so pressing. Somehow, she'd managed to put him off. But now that they were at the inn, it wouldn't be so easy.

With his black leather laptop bag slung over his shoulder, Jaxson gave her a peck on the cheek, picked up their carry-ons, and led them up the steps past the old stone fountain. Holiday held the heavy wooden doors with "W" and "M" engraved on the glass panes, and they passed into an expansive lobby with a gorgeous, oaken staircase and an enormous old registry open on a black marble desk before them. She flipped through several pages and saw years of signatures. There were no other visitors around, and the house was quiet and serene. Light classical music provided an air of dignified repose.

Jaxson dropped the suitcases. "Once we get checked in, I want to explore this old house and take pictures." His eyes were wide as he marveled at their surroundings. "Seriously, this must be the scene of our next mystery."

Past the stairs was the drawing room, or parlor, as the hotel website called it. It could have been the setting for the dénouement of an Agatha Christie novel, where Poirot finally unveils the killer's identity. Polished oak trimmed the windows and doors. A finely crafted wooden bookshelf, featuring vintage volumes, silver teapots, and an Elizabethan plate, was inset into a pale green wall. At the back of the room was a stunning gray Italian marble fireplace, accompanied by an equally impressive mirror above it. A four-shaded light fixture hung from the white ornamental plastered ceiling. And in the center of the room, gorgeous antique chairs and tables sat on a large, taupe-colored Oriental rug that spread across the beautiful, geometrical patterns of the brown parquet. Even a striking old grandfather clock stood like a sage sentry in one corner.

Jaxson draped an arm around Holiday's shoulders. "It's like something straight out of a whodunit." His eyes sparkled. "Look, there's Tiffany glass in the windows above the doors. And check out the ceiling. Doing that kind of intricate, ornamental plasterwork must've taken forever. It's got to be all original. Just beautiful."

A distant memory floated into Holiday's mind. *That ceiling looks like our wedding cake.*

"May I help you?"

A tall, middle-aged man in a black suit and tie sat at a polished oak desk in the lobby to their right. His face was clean-shaven, his hair a salt-and-pepper gray. He tapped the keyboard before an expansive monitor and studied them over small black readers perched on the end of his nose. He seemed to hunch over slightly when he rose and extended his hand.

Jaxson stepped forward. "My wife and I are checking in for the weekend. We are the Bridgewaters."

"Leonard Fairbourne is the name. Miss Southerleigh and I have been expecting you. Welcome to Wentworth Mansion. I'm the innkeeper and quite happy to assist you." Leonard had a squinty smile, and his soft, measured Carolinian accent came out like sticky syrup trickling down a stack of warm flapjacks. He pushed the black reading glasses up the bridge of his nose and invited them toward two hardwood chairs adjacent to his desk. "You are the first to arrive." His hands floated to the top of his keyboard, and his fingers moved briskly across the keys. "Give me just a moment to finish another file and find yours."

Jaxson leaned over to his wife as they waited. "Explain why you sent a text this morning asking me to fly to Charleston from DC instead of back to Dallas. I was lucky to get a seat on a flight that landed about the same time as yours."

Holiday patted his leg and winked. "All in due time, dear." She pressed her lips together and willed the knot in her stomach to loosen. It didn't.

Jaxson frowned. "That's what you said in the cab from the airport." He reached for the phone in his pocket. "Hold still!" He removed his fedora, plopped it on his wife's head, cocking it just a bit to one side, and aimed his phone at her. "I saw a beautiful picture just then." He showed her the photo. "We'll use your face for our next novel's leading lady." Jaxson wiggled his fingers as though typing on an invisible keyboard. "She had eyes that were the color of deep coral, golden hair that fell in waves just below thin shoulders, and a confident light pink smile that spread evenly across a fair face." He leaned over to her ear. "And she wore a brown leather fedora, the kind she imagined Sam Spade might wear. Or Sam Spade's girlfriend when he wasn't wearing it, or his shirt." He wiggled his eyebrows at her.

Holiday lowered her chin and gave her husband a look. "Do you mean Iva Archer, the wife of Sam's partner, with whom he was having an affair?" She rolled her eyes and shook her head. "Some partner, cheating with his best friend's wife." She took the phone from Jaxson's hand and studied the photo he'd taken. "I do like the way this hat looks."

"You'll make a great femme fatale." He leaned his forehead on hers. "Okay, back to my question. Why are we here? Give it up."

Holiday let out a long sigh through pouty lips. "I know this was sudden, but my old college friend Daily called me yesterday afternoon and asked, even on short notice, if I could get away this weekend and meet her in Charleston. She said she had something important to share about the murder of one of our friends, Bobby Boudreaux."

"Murder? Yikes." He raised his eyebrows. "She couldn't just tell you over the phone?"

Holiday shook her head. "She said it had to be where it happened."

Jaxson narrowed his gaze at her. "He was murdered here? Charleston?"

Holiday nodded. Her heart was racing.

The innkeeper cleared his throat and took off his glasses. "You will stay in Room 19, a lovely corner room on the fourth floor that overlooks our garden patio, our award-winning restaurant, Circa 1886, and our luxurious spa. And you will also be able to glimpse our charming old downtown."

Holiday's breath caught—Room 19—the same as before.

This was just like Daily. Holiday's heart pounded inside her chest, and she breathed deeply to calm herself. If she could just see Daily and get a read on her old friend's temperament, maybe she'd find the situation more benign than she feared. Perhaps Daily just wanted to reunite the old gang. Share some drinks. Laugh about the good times. And tell everyone a deep, dark secret, too?

She forced a smile. "It sounds lovely." She looked around the room. "Has Daily...arrived?"

"Miss Southerleigh arrived late last night and has spent the day preparing for your arrival and that of your friends."

Leonard stole a look at his monitor. "I believe there are eight of you checking in, including Miss Southerleigh."

"Eight?" Jaxson turned to Holiday, who gave her husband an apologetic shrug. "You didn't tell me it was a gang of people." He went back to the clerk. "How much do we owe you, Mr. Fairbourne?"

The innkeeper waved him off. "Please, call me Leonard. And there is no charge for your stay here, Mr. Bridgewater. Miss Southerleigh has already pre-paid your expenses, including your room, spa treatments, and dinner tonight and tomorrow at Circa 1886, which I believe you will find quite satisfactory. She has also requested the use of our conference room downstairs." He lowered his voice. "As you may know, Miss Southerleigh is a bit of a celebrity here in the Holy City."

"The Holy City?" Jaxson said. "And, no, I don't know."

"Our skyline is dotted by over four hundred church steeples representing many different expressions of faith." Leonard pointed to a large painting, wrapped in a thick, gilded frame, above his desk. "This neo-classical landscape is a 19th-century piece and is said to have been original to the house when Francis Silas Rodgers had it constructed for his family in the late 1880s. Miss Southerleigh was instrumental in retrieving the painting for us. It had been lost for over five decades before she tracked it down and brought it home. I suppose some people have the gift of unraveling a good mystery. This city loves its well-known artist. I suspect you might get a tour of her gallery during your stay with us this weekend." Leonard looked at his phone. "Will you two excuse me for a moment? There is a minor emergency that I must attend to. I won't be but a minute."

He jumped from his chair and headed into a room at the back of the lobby.

Jaxson turned to Holiday. "Okay, now tell me, what's going on? Why are we here? And what's this bit about a secret and a murder?"

Holiday shrugged. "She said she wanted to talk to all eight of us at the same time."

"Didn't give any hint as to what it was?"

Holiday swallowed hard. Her college friend hadn't needed to.

She shook her head. "Only that it had something to do with Bobby's death twenty years ago."

A loud crash came from the direction in which Leonard had fled, and the couple looked at each other and giggled.

"By the way," said Holiday, "how was the writing conference? Were the speakers good?"

"Excellent as always. There is another conference in Galveston in a few months, and I thought we could go to that one together. I think we should if we're going to write stories as a team. I want to do this with you, you know."

"Of course, dear, I would love that."

Jaxson checked his watch. "Okay, tell me about your friend."

Holiday shifted in her seat toward Jaxson. "Daily Southerleigh and I grew up together in Highland Park. Went to the same elementary, middle, and high school. Rode our bikes all over. Then, we went to SMU and roomed together for all four years. We even pledged the same sorority. We were thick as thieves through college. We even had our secret ways of leaving each other notes. Invisible ink. Steam on mirrors. Hard-boiled eggs. After college, she became a successful artist, and as Leonard said, she has her gallery here in..."

"Okay, I'm back," Leonard boomed as he reentered the

lobby. He was panting hard and almost running as he flailed into his chair. "Where were we?"

"You said there were eight of us arriving," Jaxson reminded. "Did Miss Southerleigh say for what reason?"

"As I understand, sir, it is a college reunion. A time of relaxation and a time for reliving those wonderful moments when all the world was before us."

Holiday could feel her stomach twisting.

A heavy-set man in his mid-thirties with a black shaggy mop of hair appeared from a room down the hall. His black slacks and white button-down matched his plain and unassuming demeanor. The thin black patch under his chin gave him a passé beatnik look. He nodded when he saw the Bridgewaters.

Leonard stood and handed the couple two square brass keys. "This is Geoffrey. He will be assisting you to Room 19."

"Actual keys." Jaxson compared his key to Holiday's. "Can you believe it? I love this place already."

"All the door fixtures are exactly as they were when Wentworth Mansion was constructed in 1886," said Leonard. "Our current owners painstakingly remodeled our beautiful mansion back to the vision Mr. Rodgers had for it when he dreamed of a wonderful home for his wife and children. Of course, there are a few modern conveniences now, such as the elevator located in the center of our grand staircase, but much of its charm remains unchanged. We hope you will find your stay at Wentworth Mansion peaceful and luxurious. Your first scheduled activity for the weekend is a couple's massage at four o'clock. You will find our award-winning spa behind the main building in what once was the mansion's stables. It's next door to Circa 1886."

Holiday drew in a deep breath and looked around the

lobby. "It's just beautiful, this old inn. It has so much character. Just delightful."

"Character and history." Leonard clasped his hands in front of him. "We like to think of Wentworth Mansion as a lifelong friend with whom you will always feel comfortable, a family member with whom you will want to visit again and again. I don't mind telling you our guests report that they learn more about our worthy friend with each visit. They get more acquainted with her. Perhaps it's a bit presumptuous on my part, but I like to think that with each visit, Wentworth also becomes more intimate with its visitors."

"I hope these walls can't talk." Holiday grimaced. "It could be embarrassing what they might say."

Jaxson raised a single finger to his lips. "What happens in the Holy City stays in the Holy City. Right?" He slipped his wife a wink.

Leonard chuckled. "I am convinced that if the walls of Wentworth could speak, they would whisper, 'Your story is safe with me.'" He smiled, his eyes squinting. "I've always found that the safest people and places are the ones with the deepest wounds. Abuse. Abandonment. Neglect. Wentworth has had her share of pain. It's what makes her inviting. She understands."

Holiday frowned.

I prefer this wonderful old inn to have a short memory.

And what about Leonard? Did he know something about Holiday? Had Daily said something to him? She eyed the innkeeper and made a mental note to be careful around him.

Jaxson glanced at his watch. "We'd better get to our room if we have massages in an hour."

"Indeed, you should." Leonard extended his hand

toward the concierge. "I will turn you over to the competent hands of our good man, Geoffrey."

Geoffrey smiled and nodded. Jaxson and Holiday thanked Leonard and followed the concierge to the elevator. Jaxson stepped into the parlor and ran his hand along the grandfather clock.

"I mean, seriously," he said, "doesn't this place make you want to play a game of *Clue*?" He looked at his watch. "The clock is exactly one hour behind."

Geoffrey stood beside him. "That clock hasn't run in years, not since I've been here." His voice was soft and high-pitched.

Holiday cocked her head to take in the ceiling, then turned away before Jaxson could notice.

The elevator door opened, and a woman in her 80s, wearing a wine-colored bow cloche, exited the carriage. She wielded a beige walking cane in one hand and an unadorned brown purse in the other.

"You look so pretty," Holiday said to her. "I love your hat."

The woman tipped it to her. "Thank you, young lady. I hope I'm not too late for afternoon wine and hors d'oeuvres in the sunroom."

Geoffrey assured her she was very much on time and ushered Jaxson and Holiday into the small elevator. He pushed button four, and the trio began their climb to the top floor.

Holiday thought about the predicament between her and Daily. What if she just bared her soul to her and came clean about what happened between her and Bobby that night? They'd been privy to each other's deepest secrets and regrets for the first half of their lives. Not that they hadn't hurt each other from time to time. But they'd always kept a short leash on their grudges. Forgiveness had always been quickly asked for and promptly given.

Twenty years ago.

All at once, the elevator stopped, bouncing slightly, and the car was thrown into darkness.

"Nothing to fear," Geoffrey said. "It happens from time to time. Probably just one of our friendly ghosts messing around."

Holiday sighed. Daily. She was doing it again.

In the blackness of the carriage, Holiday searched for any red blinking light of a hidden camera in the elevator's ceiling. Was Daily watching them now? Controlling, manipulating, the same as she'd always done back then? She closed her eyes to the darkness around her. She couldn't let her old friend get to her. She needed to begin anticipating what Daily might do. Next time, she and Jaxson would take the stairs.

Daily had maneuvered Holiday back to Wentworth Mansion.

She'd booked her in Room 19.

And now she'd trapped her in the elevator.

Daily was replaying every detail from the night Bobby had died.

The night Holiday had sent Daily's fiancé toward his death in Wentworth's Grand Mansion Suite.

Holiday felt her husband's hands slip around her waist. It would be different this time. Jaxson was with her, and he would help her.

Discover. Deny. Bury.

"Dear, I want to discuss something with you when we get to the room." She reached for Jaxson's hand and gripped it tightly. "Something you should know about Daily."

"Nothing too serious, I hope."

"Well, I guess it kind of is," she said, her voice cagey.

He pressed his lips to the top of her head. "We'll talk about it as soon as we are rescued."

Jaxson. The love of her life. Her partner in crime writing. And the man who was going to help her bury her past.

All she had to do was keep him from knowing what he was helping her bury.

A shudder ran down her spine. She'd lost her best friend twenty years ago by hiding a secret. She couldn't afford to lose her new husband over the same secret.

2

———

The lights came back on in less than a minute, and the elevator continued to the top floor.

Holiday sprinted through the lines she'd memorized during her flight to CHS. In a moment, she and Jaxson would be alone in their room. She needed to fully embed him in her plan to convince Daily of her innocence, which meant sharing select details of that night twenty years ago. The details that didn't reveal all the facts.

She took a deep breath and turned to the concierge. "Are there ghosts at Wentworth?"

"That's what people say, but I've worked here for almost ten years and I've never seen one. Some say it's the ghosts of visitors who once lodged here. Others say it's the ghost of one of Mr. Rodgers's thirteen children."

Holiday glanced at Jaxson and smiled. Every old hotel with character had a ghost story.

"You must be the resident hotel historian," she said to the concierge.

Jaxson winked at Holiday. "I love a good history lesson."

Geoffrey continued. "Mr. Rodgers was quite wealthy. He was a cotton merchant, and when he commissioned the building of this home, he insisted there be a room for each child. There was also a school room so that the children might be educated. Downstairs, you'll find a beautiful library just past the parlor. There's a history of the mansion, as well as a desktop computer, board games, and books. Down the hall from your room on the fourth floor is the spiral staircase to the cupola. You must go up there at some point during your stay. There are spectacular views of historic Charleston from every angle." He paused. "Um, the library and the cupola are the two places at Wentworth where people claim to see spirits. Of course, if you ask me, the only ghosts that ever inhabit Wentworth Mansion are the ones its guests bring with them."

Jaxson took a deep breath and patted Geoffrey on the back. "We'll be on the lookout for any paranormal activity this weekend."

The elevator bell chimed, the door opened, and Geoffrey led them to the room across the hall.

"Here we are." Geoffrey waited until Jaxson opened the door, followed them in, and set their suitcases on the floor. "As you can see, you have your own fireplace. Feel free to use it. It's been converted to gas, so it is quite convenient." Geoffrey opened the luggage racks as he spoke and set up their carry-ons. "Your bathroom has a tub and a walk-in shower. Please let us know if you need anything at all, and we will be more than happy to assist you." Geoffrey opened the door and waited. "Any questions?"

Jaxson and Holiday shook their heads.

"I think you answered them all." Jaxson chuckled. "Even the ones we didn't know we had."

The room was precisely as Holiday had remembered:

rich, patterned wallpaper, an ornate, intricately carved four-poster bed, and heavy, red velvet drapes.

Jaxson handed Geoffrey a generous tip. The concierge nodded and closed the door behind him.

Jaxson pulled a box of yellow Sprite Tic Tacs from his shirt pocket, popped a few of the candies in his mouth, and set the box on the writing table next to the bed. "Okay, love, now finish telling me about this murder business. There might be a mystery here I can use in our next book."

Holiday gave him a playful shove. "Don't even think about it, mister."

They settled into matching brown jacquard Queen Anne-style armchairs in front of the unlit marble fireplace.

"When you marry," Holiday's mother had once told her, "remember the words my mother said to me on the eve of my wedding: Your husband will only be as angry as the secrets you choose to remember. Forgiveness is a costly balm in a marriage that has lost its tenderness. And, my dear, they all lose their tenderness. Better to be forgetful than remorseful."

In other words, keep the really bad stuff to herself.

Growing up, Holiday couldn't recall a tender moment between her parents, and she'd told herself she would never have a marriage built on secrets. That was one reason she'd waited until her forties to get married. And, still, here she was.

Her mother's voice pierced her thoughts. "You don't want the sins of your past to wreak havoc on the success of your present. Protect your marriage, Holi, at all costs."

Discover. Deny. Bury.

With some help from Jaxson.

"Bobby Boudreaux was a friend in college," Holiday said

carefully, "and when he met Daily, there was an instant spark."

"Love at first sight? That's exactly the way it was for me when I met you at the Driskill in Austin. I couldn't keep my eyes off you. Still can't." He threw his head back. "Oh, my gosh, remember that first night we explored the hotel?"

"How could I forget?" Holiday laughed. "I can't believe we didn't get caught!"

"I fell in love with you right then." He squeezed her hand. "Okay, back to your story about Bobby and Daily."

Holiday gave him a smart salute. "They got engaged, but something changed, and he broke it off. He said he was going to Charleston. And…"

Jaxson leaned his head forward. "And?"

And…and…and…

"And that was the last time she heard from him. He was killed here at Wentworth. His murder was never solved. I was stunned. The whole gang was."

"Is this the group that we are meeting this weekend?"

Holiday nodded. "There were eight of us in all. We called ourselves the Crazy Eights."

"Like the card game?"

"Right." Holiday got two bottles of Diet Coke from the fridge in the armoire and offered one to Jaxson. "In October, just a few months after we graduated, Bobby took a trip to Charleston. The next time Daily saw him, he was in a casket in Dallas."

"How tragic. That must've done a number on her."

"I don't think she ever got over it. Of all the places in the world for her to establish herself as an artist, she chose the very place where the love of her life was killed." Holiday stood and flipped a switch behind the drapes to turn on the fireplace in the room. A gas flame immediately filled the small brick alcove.

"That is odd. You'd think this would be the last place she'd want to live," he said. "So, what's up with having everyone meet here? Is she telling everyone this secret of hers or just you?"

"All of us, I guess." Holiday shrugged. "She said she wanted to get the whole gang together and reveal what she's figured out. She said it was a Crazy Eights weekend at Wentworth Mansion, all expenses paid. So that's when I asked you to fly here instead of back to Dallas. And I was curious who would and wouldn't accept the invitation as sudden as it was, but she texted me last night saying everyone was coming."

"Wow. I'm impressed they could get away so quickly, but good for them." Jaxson downed the rest of his bottle and tossed it neatly in the trash can beneath the black antique desk. "Tell me about these people."

"Daily can be off-putting at first until you get to know her. She's a strong, goal-minded woman. Don't get in her way. Then there's Beau Culverhouse, who lives in Houston. Last I heard, he's a headhunter in the oil and gas market. There's Michael Herrington. He also lives in Houston. He's in the restaurant industry now, I think. There's Tú Dinh, who is...well...hmm...how should I put this?" Holiday tapped the side of her bottle as she thought. "She was studying to be a lawyer, quit, and now I don't know what she does. I think she stays at home." Holiday bit her lip. "It may be a bit awkward seeing her again."

"Why?"

Holiday grimaced. "We didn't end on the best of notes. This whole thing with Bobby finished the Crazy Eights."

Jaxson nodded and recounted the people on his fingers. "That's four, not counting you."

"And finally, there's the happy couple."

"You and me," Jaxson said.

Holiday laughed. "Dave and Payton Bell. They dated in high school, all through college, and got married before graduation. They've got four kids, all girls. And she records every happy thing they do on social media. They are an *extremely happy couple* if you know what I mean."

"Like, over-the-top happy?"

"Very. Payton posts everything about her life. What she wore, what she made for the kids' lunches, and how happy they were to attend school. She posts their sporting events with the kids. Their vacations. Their...everything. Lots and lots of pictures with everyone posing. Always smiling. Always happy."

Jaxson nodded. "What about Dave? Same thing?"

"No. He posts nothing. He's in the pictures. Sometimes, he's smiling. But it's all Payton."

"A reunion of the Crazy Eights," said Jaxson.

"Yes." Holiday gave him a pouty lip. "Minus one. Bobby Boudreaux. And I must tell you, it's bizarre that Daily is having us meet here in Charleston this weekend. Tomorrow is the twentieth anniversary of Bobby's murder."

"Are you serious? This very weekend?" Jaxson narrowed his eyes. "That is strange. Why hasn't this been solved already? What did the police find out?"

Holiday shrugged. "There was no evidence that anyone at the inn killed Bobby. The police said it was most likely a random act of violence. The accessibility of Bobby's room on the main floor. The inn's unlocked front door." She shook her head. "Daily never bought it. And now we're all here again after two decades. I wish I knew why."

"She probably just wants to bring you all here to remember the good old days," Jaxson said, "and to make the memory of Bobby a part of it as well, since it is the anniversary weekend."

Holiday frowned. "That wouldn't be like Daily. She doesn't do social unless something is to be gained." She shook her head. "This secret of hers—she found something about Bobby, and now she wants to tell everyone what it is."

Jaxson stood and grabbed his coat. "We've got thirty minutes before our massages. I'm going to explore the grounds a bit and take some photos. You want to come?" He scooped up the box of Tic Tacs and dropped them in his shirt pocket.

Holiday stood and kissed him. "No, thank you, dear. I have plenty of unpacking, and I'd like some alone time before the evening gets busy with the rest of the gang."

"Very well, baby. I won't be gone long."

Jaxson gave her a quick kiss and left. Holiday began to unpack.

She could feel a pit in her stomach. What was Daily planning?

She and Daily had been as close as sisters throughout the first half of their lives. Daily had told Holiday every little secret about her relationship with Bobby. But when he broke the engagement, things changed between the two friends. Bobby wanted to date Holiday, and he'd told Daily, too.

Holiday was the one Bobby was seeing in Charleston the weekend he was killed. They had stayed together in the same beautiful old inn. In the same beautiful Room 19.

She's recreating the murder. And she still blames me.

Holiday could've declined her invitation to the weekend reunion. It was all so last-minute. She could've said she had something else planned, Jaxson was out of town, or her father needed help with his candy company.

But no, she had to come and return to the scene of the crime, as it were. Twenty years was long enough for the suspicions to endure. It was time to prove to Daily that she wasn't the one who'd killed Bobby Boudreaux.

"Even though I did."

Historic Charleston was spectacular from the wooden deck that encircled the brilliant white and red domed cupola atop the old mansion. The cupola was like an upside-down onion, its root the steeple, among many others in the Holy City. What a remarkable idea to include a space at the top of one's home to view the historic downtown streets where the earliest residents had lived, and the Charleston Harbor that lay just beyond. Was that Fort Sumter in the distance? Everywhere he saw dozens of beautiful white steeples, uneven cobblestone streets, and gorgeous magnolia trees with stunning white blooms.

From the moment they'd arrived, Jaxson knew he and Holiday would use the house as the setting of a story. But he needed photographs to remember its Victorian Gothic features. Down the hall from their room, he'd discovered the wrought iron spiraling staircase leading up to the cupola, and it was there that he'd begun his photographic hunt.

A waist-high glass retaining wall encircled the cupola along the deck's perimeter. It wouldn't have been there in 1886. Perhaps there'd been some other way to keep Mr. Rodgers's thirteen children from falling to their deaths. The deck had a trap door on the mansion's north side to access the air conditioning units on the other side of the glass partitions. Jaxson counted twenty white flues extending from five separate brick chimneys. The house had a lot of fireplaces.

The door to the cupola opened and closed. Perhaps Holiday had decided to explore after all? When nobody appeared, he decided it was just the draft through the house that had caught the door.

He took pictures of the skyline and the grounds before retreating inside. The cupola's arching white windows lit up the spiraling staircase to the fourth floor. He took some additional photos of the circling wooden steps. One didn't often see that kind of fixture in houses, and he might need to reference it later if he set one of his and Holiday's mysteries in the old inn.

A man and a woman's argument drifted up to him from below. He wanted to peek over the railing of the stairs, but with only twenty-one rooms at Wentworth, it was likely he'd run into them again, and he didn't want to make it awkward. Instead, he flattened himself against the windows and listened.

"This is your fault," the woman said. "You were the one who gave her the idea by asking if she'd found anything new."

"Seriously? That's absurd. I was asking what the rest of us wanted to know. We don't need something from twenty years ago wrecking our chances for everything we have now. We need to know what she knows."

Was this the "happy couple" Holiday had mentioned? Dave and Payton?

"Trust me, we're all gonna find out what she knows."

The woman sighed, and again, Jaxson tried leaning over

to catch a glimpse of the couple, but they were too far below for him to see.

"You could've said no." The man's voice was softer.

The woman snickered. "I see you're here, too. Don't tell me you think this is just a college reunion. She knows something. It's different this time. She's different." The woman paused, and there was light tapping on the metal railing. "It's almost as though she's testing us, waiting to see who's gonna give first."

"She was always so much drama."

"Why do you think Bobby dumped her?"

Were they talking about the same Bobby who had been killed in the mansion? If Jaxson could only see their faces.

He tried again to see them, but his foot skidded across something slick, and he tipped over the railing. He caught himself just in time, but his box of Tic Tacs hurtled out of his pocket and into the stairwell, colliding with several steps before landing at the bottom.

Jaxson threw himself back against the windows and held his breath. The couple was sure to run up the stairs and discover him. But all Jaxson could hear were muffled whispers and quick paces down the hall toward the elevator. Jaxson eased over the railing, peering into the dim hole below.

They were gone, along with his box of Tic Tacs. Whoever they'd been, they'd taken his breath mints with them.

3

———

"How can I be expected to return to reality after all that amazing relaxation?" Jaxson rolled to his side on the massage therapist's table.

Holiday stretched her arms above her head. "I'm surprised you remember how relaxing your massage was, dear."

"What do you mean?"

"You might've slept through the majority of it."

"I didn't snore, did I?"

She gave him a wink. "Maybe only a little."

Holiday wished she could've relaxed and prepared for a sublime evening at the most romantic inn. But as still as she had been during the massage, her mind had run a mile a minute. If Daily was indeed going to confront her about Bobby's death, Holiday would need to find a way to sidestep her accusations.

She dug out from under the heavy sheets on the massage table and slipped into her plush, white robe, tying the sash around her slim waist.

"I suppose we should think about returning to our room

and cleaning up for dinner." Jaxson pushed his arms through the sleeves of his robe. "By the way, I overheard an argument while I was at the top of the cupola today." He scooted his feet into the black, heavy rubber slippers. "There was a couple at the bottom of the spiral stairs—it's so beautiful up there, you'll have to come with me to see it—anyway, I didn't get a look at them, but they were arguing about...Well, about being here. I mean, it sounded like someone you might know."

"Me?" Holiday slipped into her sandals. "What were their names?"

"I don't know, but they knew Daily. And they seemed to know all about Bobby, too."

"You didn't see who they were?"

Jaxson shook his head. "It seems they felt compelled to be here. They were none too happy about the whole thing."

"I know exactly how they feel," Holiday muttered.

"What?"

"I said, 'I'm starving.'" She kissed him. "Let's go to dinner."

Jaxson glanced at his phone. "We'd better hurry. We have just over an hour to get ready, and if you're going to do your whole routine with your hair, we'd better get going."

Dinner. It would be the first time she'd seen Daily in twenty years. Her pulse quickened. She'd seen photos of Daily as she read the artist's story from obscurity to one of Charleston's most famous residents. Holiday had often wondered if Daily ever thought of her. Maybe she had gotten too well-known, too important to care about old relationships. Shockingly, everyone had been able to make it, as if they'd all known it was coming but her. It could only mean one thing. Nobody wanted to miss the drama when Daily pointed the finger at Holiday.

But Holiday came armed with Jaxson. A handsome man with a beautiful soul, the kind of husband any woman would want. They would see Jaxson and view her differently. They would doubt their memories, the rumors, the gossip, and Holiday would make them believe that whatever Daily said about her, the truth was something else. And Jaxson would back her up.

Her stomach felt like one big knot. She drew a long breath and steeled herself.

Back outside their room, Holiday shook her hair loose. "I am so ready to wash this rat's nest of mine."

"Need any help?" Jaxson opened the door and held it for her. "If you haven't noticed, the shower is just the right size for two."

"Not a chance. If I let you in there, we'll never get to dinner tonight." She patted his cheek and placed a light kiss on his lips. "But if I need you, I'll call you."

From outside the room came a loud thud, as if something heavy had fallen.

"Oh, my God, I think I broke it!" a man shouted.

Jaxson looked at Holiday, then at the grand staircase. "Hello?" he called out.

Holiday looked over the railing that wrapped around behind the elevator. "Did someone fall down the stairs?"

"Over here! At the bottom of the cupola," the man said with a strangled voice.

The couple darted down the short hall and found a rugged man with bronze skin, dressed in bright green golf shorts and a white polo, at the bottom of the spiral staircase. His ruddy hair was pulled back in a man-bun, and he was sitting up and clutching his ankle.

"I think I broke it. It hurts like a—"

"Beau?" Holiday said. "Is that you? Oh my gosh, are you okay?"

Holiday had been so fixated on Daily that she hadn't thought about how it might feel to see the other members of the Crazy Eights after two decades. She slipped her hands into her pockets. They were shaking.

Beau grabbed the banister, tried pulling up, winced, and slumped to the floor.

"Easy there," Jaxson said. "Let me help you. We'd better have someone examine that foot."

Holiday smiled at her husband. Already, Jaxson was showing himself to be the kind of man they would admire, and the type of man who would marry a woman they could admire, too.

"What happened, Beau?" Holiday asked, placing a comforting hand on his arm.

Jaxson looked at the top of the spiral staircase and back at Beau. "Did you fall down these stairs?"

Beau hung his head. "Like a veritable idiot." He nodded to the top of the cupola. "There's something slippery up there on the floor. I noticed it when I went up, but forgot about it on the way down. I guess I hit it just right, and here I am. I can't believe I broke my foot, ankle, whatever on the first day we're here." He smiled at Holiday. "Hi, beautiful. Long time no see."

"I almost went over the railing up there, too." Jaxson extended his hand to Beau. "I'm Jaxson."

"Beau, Jaxson is my husband." Holiday placed a hand on Jaxson's shoulder. "Dear, this is Beau Culverhouse, one of the infamous members of the Crazy Eights."

"And the clumsiest one," Beau said. "You got yourself a fine woman there, Jax."

"Where does it hurt?" Jaxson asked.

Beau jumped as Jaxson prodded his foot and ankle. "Take it easy there, friend."

Jaxson tried moving the foot at the ankle, but Beau clenched his teeth and pulled away. At last, the couple helped the man hoist himself and then assisted him in hobbling to the elevator.

"You would know I'm on the second floor," Beau said as they took the elevator to his room. "Gonna be tough getting in and out of this place with all the steps."

"Maybe Leonard can put you on the ground floor to make it easier," Jaxson suggested. "Once we get you settled, I'll talk to Leonard about moving you." He eyed Beau's ankle and frowned. "There's no discoloration. Still, probably wouldn't hurt to get it looked at."

Beau waved off the suggestion. "Before I go traipsing off to some hospital and racking up a bill for no reason, I'm gonna see if Leonard has one of those doctors that still makes house calls."

The elevator dinged as the trio reached the second floor.

"Are you sure about that?" Jaxson asked. "Might be good to get it X-rayed."

"I will if the doctor suggests it."

The three hobbled out of the elevator into Beau's room. They got Beau to bed and propped up his legs.

Jaxson left to talk to Leonard, and Beau turned to Holiday. "I bet you were surprised to hear from Daily after all these years."

Holiday went to the window closest to the fireplace and counted four church steeples. The Holy City. Was that why she was feeling so judged? And then a thought flashed in her mind. She didn't have to wait until dinner to build her defense. Beau had already met Jaxson. Winning Beau over now would make building her defense with the others much easier at dinner.

"Surprise was not the word for it. More like shocked." Holiday sat on the edge of the bed near Beau's feet.

"I hope you don't mind me asking, but does she still blame you?" asked Beau.

The man was about as subtle as a minidress at a funeral.

She sighed deeply and shrugged. "Hard to say. We didn't speak long on the phone last night, and I haven't seen her today." She looked at her phone. Thirty minutes until dinner. Showers would have to wait until later that night. "I'm eager to catch up with everyone. And I'm excited for you all to meet Jaxson. He is such an amazing husband. I can tell the two of you will hit it off marvelously."

Beau was undeterred. "Didn't she tell you?"

Holiday feigned momentary confusion. "Oh, you mean, Daily." She shrugged again. "I assumed it was to remember the twentieth anniversary of Bobby's passing."

Beau gave her a side eye. "She told me she had some new information about that night."

Daily had told them all the same thing. But maybe she'd told the others more. Perhaps she had mentioned Holiday. Did they all know something she didn't?

"She knows who killed Bobby?"

Beau raised his hands. "I didn't say that. She just said it would close this chapter in her life."

Holiday pictured herself walking into the Circa 1886 restaurant, unaware that everyone was waiting, like a circle of friends at an intervention, ready to break her down and get her to confess to first-degree murder.

"Close this chapter? Do you mean Charleston? Is she moving away?"

"All she said to me was..."

The door to the room opened, and Jaxson and Leonard appeared.

"Leonard is going to move you to the Grand Mansion Suite," Jaxson announced. "It's not on the ground floor, but at least it'll put you on the floor with the parlor, library, and sunroom, and you can take the elevator down to the ground. Best of all, you get the most amazing room in the mansion. Lucky dog." He looked at Beau's foot. "Well, sort of..."

"You say there's something slippery at the top of the cupola? I will address this straight away." Leonard rolled a wheelchair next to the bed. "If you will assist me, Mr. Bridgewater, we can get our good friend to his new room with as little discomfort as possible."

Leonard pushed Beau in the wheelchair, and Jaxson struggled with Beau's extra-large suitcase.

"I think you packed more than one sink in this behemoth," Jaxson said.

Beau laughed. "I never know what I'll need, so I tend to bring it all."

Jaxson and Holiday took the stairs so the elevator could accommodate Leonard and Beau. On each floor's landing, Jaxson set the suitcase down and took a quick breather.

"And you say my suitcase is heavy!" Holiday teased her husband.

"I will never complain again about the way you pack." Jaxson lifted the suitcase, and they continued down the steps.

Leonard let everyone into the Grand Mansion Suite on the main floor, and the two men assisted Beau to the bed. The room, a marvel of Victorian affluence, was a single space running the entire width of the mansion, with separate sleeping and living areas, divided by two large wooden pocket doors. A marble fireplace stood at each end of the room, and the floor had an exquisitely intricate warm brown parquet pattern. The most gorgeous chandeliers Holiday had ever seen hung in the center of each living space.

She closed her eyes and felt her stomach turn. This room was also just as she'd remembered.

"This had to be the master bedroom." Jaxson walked to the back of the suite and took in the large bathroom.

"Actually, the front room was originally the men's smoking room. Where we are standing was where the ladies met. Strict societal rules during the Victorian age prohibited the frequent mixing of the sexes." He pointed to the chande-liers. "Original to the house, along with the marble bust on the fireplace mantle behind Mrs. Bridgewater."

Beau whistled. "This actually might've been worth breaking my ankle."

"As per your request, sir," said Leonard, "Dr. Miller should be here in five to ten minutes. He has been a good friend to Wentworth Mansion for decades."

"We'll wait with you until the doctor arrives," Jaxson offered.

Holiday closed her eyes and found herself unable to breathe. There was nowhere in the room she wanted to look.

"Dear, it's been a long day, and I think I'm going to head to our room." She smiled weakly at Beau. "It's lovely to see you again, my friend. I hope you get wonderful news from the doctor." She turned toward the door but, as an afterthought, added, "Let Jaxson or me know if you need anything. He's like you. He has the most wonderful heart."

"Don't worry about a thing," Beau called after Holiday as she left the room. "Jax and I are gonna have a wonderful talk while we wait."

Holiday thought about Beau's words as she dragged

herself up the grand staircase and retreated to Room 19. Jaxson would vouch for her. Any doubts Beau had of Holiday would be dispelled as Jaxson told Beau what a wonderful wife Holiday was. She nodded to herself. This was why she had needed Jaxson there with her. He would be her advocate.

Ten minutes later, Jaxson entered their room and announced that the house physician was with Beau. Holiday decided not to ask what Beau had told him.

"I suppose we don't have time to shower before dinner, dear." Holiday slipped out of her top and pants. "I'll have to do my hair routine after we eat."

The two changed and took the grand staircase to the main floor and out the inn's back door to Circa 1886. Holiday wore a black slip dress, and Jaxson wore black jeans, a white-collared button-down, and a blue dinner jacket with a black lapel.

Her heart pounded, and she tried to breathe deeply as the inky blackness of the night settled over Charleston, like the foreboding cloud of dread settling over her mind. Would Daily get right to it or prolong Holiday's agony and make her case against her old friend after dessert had been served and eaten? Holiday felt like a prisoner going for her last meal, and she gripped her husband's hand tighter.

"It's quite odd how it worked out," said Jaxson. "With your friend Beau, I mean."

His words pulled her mind out of despair. "Who knows what that slippery mess was?" she said. "Probably just some kid's melted popsicle. It happens. Hopefully, Beau gets good news from the doctor."

"No, that's not what I meant," Jaxson said.

Holiday gave him a puzzled look.

"The Grand Mansion Suite," he continued, "where Beau

is now. When I went down to inquire about moving Beau, Leonard said the room had been reserved, but someone called to cancel the reservation about an hour ago. He made it sound very unusual. Then, Beau falls, and the room I suggested is conveniently available."

"You suggested a room on the ground floor," Holiday reminded.

"Still, doesn't it seem odd that Beau gets moved into the inn's most amazing room at the last second? Leonard said it was extraordinarily fortunate for Beau. People book it up months in advance."

Holiday's mind flashed back twenty years. Had Bobby booked the Grand Mansion Suite in advance when he booked Room 19?

"What are you saying?" she asked.

"It almost seems somebody wanted Beau in the room closest to the front door."

"Like a premeditated plan?" She lowered her chin at him. "You're not suggesting Beau's life is in danger, are you? Someone deliberately caused him to fall to move him to the main floor to...I don't know, do something terrible to him?"

Jaxson shrugged. "It seems to me somebody wanted Beau in the most accessible room at the inn."

Holiday shook her head. "You're talking nonsense, dear. Why would someone want to hurt Beau? It was just an unfortunate accident and a fortunate coincidence that the very room he needed opened when he needed it. Some might say he's just living right."

Jaxson held the back door and let her pass through to the outside steps as they headed toward the restaurant across the back lawn. "It's not out of the realm of possibility that someone poured something slippery on the floor so

Beau would fall and, when he did, released a room to move him into a kill zone with better access."

"Kill zone?" Holiday released her grip on her husband's hand. "Keep that cryptic plot in mind for your next book, dear."

Jaxson shrugged. "Maybe you're right. It could've been me slipping down the stairs today, breaking my leg, and ending up in the Grand Mansion Suite."

Holiday looked up at her husband.

"That slippery stuff on the floor up there. I slipped in it, too."

"You did? I thought you just tripped. You stepped in the same slime?"

Jaxson nodded. "Almost went headfirst over the rail. Caught myself in the nick of time. Lost my box of Tic Tacs, too. I guess it was the couple arguing who picked it up."

Holiday stopped at the entrance to the restaurant. "Wait. You slipped on the same stuff up there just before our massages today?"

"I think someone went up there while I was outside on the deck that wraps around the cupola and spilled something. I heard the door open and close, but never saw anyone. The slippery stuff wasn't on the floor until I returned inside." He whistled. "I could've eaten it today if I'd gone over that railing, worse than your friend Beau."

Jaxson's theory was reasonable with a tiny change.

It wasn't Beau who was meant to fall down the spiral staircase and stay in the inn's most luxurious guest room. It was her and Jaxson.

Or maybe it was me.

Someone had wanted Holiday in the same room where Bobby died.

The same room where she had found him dead.
The same room where she had drugged him.

4

None of the other Crazy Eights were in the restaurant when they arrived, but their table was ready, and Holiday formed a quick strategy. She sat Jaxson and her on one end of the table, Jaxson by the wall, and her to his left on the corner by the window. From where they sat, they had a prime view of the room's entrance. Maybe, if Holiday had a few extra seconds to judge Daily's entrance, it would reveal what kind of state the artist was in. Would Daily make eye contact with her? Would she sit beside her? Would there be folders or some incriminating evidence in her hands?

Holiday drew a deep breath and placed her hands in her lap.

It would figure that the story of what Holiday had done had to come out as it had begun: over a meal. It would be so like Daily to dig the point a little deeper.

"Are we the only ones eating?" Jaxson gestured at the long, empty table before them. "Perhaps we should be on opposite ends with a great candelabra between us."

Holiday checked her phone. "They're probably just

running a little late." She placed a hand on her chest. Her heart was pounding.

A shadow fell across the table. Michael Herrington was a large man with a wave of ginger hair combed to one side, a matching beard, and a thick mustache that shrouded his face. He loomed over them in a tight-fitting white button-down and blue jeans, his massive hand holding a beer.

Holiday smiled. "Hello, Michael." Her voice quivered as she forced the words. "It's good to see you."

"Holiday." Michael nodded at her, then at Jaxson, before sitting at the opposite end of the table.

Jaxson raised a brow to his wife. "And so, it begins."

Holiday studied her old friend. It seemed he'd always worn facial hair, even back in college, which gave him an ageless look. "That was so awkward," she whispered. "We haven't seen each other in twenty years, and he literally didn't say two words."

Jaxson squeezed her hand. "He's probably nervous. I'm sure everyone will be."

Holiday watched Michael scroll through his phone. When he looked up at her, she looked away. And when she looked at him again, he returned to his phone. She closed her eyes and drew in a long breath.

Dave and Payton Bell entered, stopping at the bar. She was smiling, her eyes wide, and wore a long, low-cut, dark green floral-print dress and a white sun hat. Dave had very dark skin and a short afro and wore black slacks and a black tee.

"The happy couple?" Jaxson whispered as the pair greeted the bartender just inside the front door.

Holiday nodded. "Last I heard, he's an accountant with a hedge fund firm in San Antonio." She watched as Payton took several selfies with the bartender. "She's a stay-at-home mom."

With drinks in hand, the Bells made their way to the table, Payton nodding and smiling at the other diners. She squealed when she saw Holiday and threw her arms around Holiday's neck. "My old friend, it's so good to see you!"

Jaxson stood so the men could shake hands.

"First time out here?" Dave asked.

Jaxson nodded. "Can you get over this beautiful old inn? Exactly the kind of house I'd love to have."

"It's haunted, you know," Dave said.

"Oh, stop it." Payton gave her husband a look. "Jaxson's right. The place is just charming." She spun and took one of Holiday's hands in her own. "And let me see that ring, girl! Oh, I love it! The man must've spent a fortune on it."

Dave sat next to Jaxson, across from Holiday. Payton took the chair next to him.

"Hey, hey, hey!" Beau entered with a crutch beneath each arm and a black orthopedic boot on his foot.

Payton squealed again. "Oh, my God, what happened to you?"

Michael smirked. "Probably broke it chasing after some—."

"You be nice, Michael Herrington!" Payton reached across the table to give Michael a playful slap on the arm.

As Beau was relating his accident to the group, Tú Dinh entered wearing a black straw bucket hat and a black N95 mask. Her long, jet-black hair matched her black cat-eye sunglasses and long black dress.

Tú took one look at Beau and waved him off, sitting at the corner next to Michael. "I don't even want to know."

"How are you, Tú?" Dave asked.

"If having a migraine every day of your life while your

kid's college drains your bank account dry is good, then I'm doing great." Tú threw her sunglasses to the table, adjusted her hat and mask, and turned to Holiday. "I wondered if you would show, considering everything that happened." She cocked her head and raised an eyebrow.

Holiday swallowed hard and let her hand slip over to Jaxson's. Tú had always had a bit of a bite to her words, which probably would've made her a decent attorney had she continued in law school. Still, she seemed more bitter and jaded, even for her. The sooner she could introduce her to Jaxson, the sooner Tú would realize Holiday wasn't that same young woman who'd had to be rescued all those years ago.

"That was a long time ago," Beau said, handing his crutches to an annoyed Michael as he wrestled himself into the chair Payton had pulled out. "Water under the bridge, as they say. I do not doubt that Daily has moved on from all that negative energy she loved stirring up."

Tú snickered. "You'd be pissed too if your best friend—."

"I see you're still wearing a mask," Payton said.

"I lost count of how many times I got Covid." Tú rolled her eyes. "I don't trust the air anymore. Where is our guest of honor, anyway?"

Dave leaned over to Jaxson. "The Crazy Eights. Emphasis on the crazy."

"It's just like Daily to be late," Michael said. "Get us all here at the last second and then keep us waiting while she's arranging paintbrushes."

The front door opened, and Holiday's heart skipped a beat, but it wasn't Daily. It was Leonard.

"I'm sorry to intrude on your evening," he said, "but Miss Southerleigh asked me to deliver this to you."

The innkeeper handed Jaxson a white envelope, nodded at the group, and left through the bar.

"We've got mail," Jaxson said.

Holiday read aloud the beautiful script across the front of the envelope.

For Jaxson and Holiday

Tú scoffed.

Jaxson handed the envelope to Holiday. "Well, that's quite mysterious," he said.

Holiday tore it open. "Can't make dinner," she read to the group. "There's one more item I must take care of before our twenty-year reunion officially begins. Please give my regards to the others. See you in the morning."

Holiday's face felt warm. First, the room. Then the dinner. Now, Daily had ghosted her. Daily's plan was becoming more apparent. She wanted to embarrass Holiday and do to Holiday what Holiday had done to her all those years ago. Holiday lowered her eyes and folded the note in half, slipping it into the pocket of her dress.

"That's odd," Jaxson said.

Tú looked from face to face. "Odd? That's putting it mildly."

"Like I said. It's just like Daily to get us all here and keep us waiting." Michael shook out his napkin and placed it in his lap. "Who's hungry? I'm starved!"

One of Beau's crutches fell on him, and he cursed it.

Payton turned to her husband. "Didn't Leonard say she was setting up a conference room downstairs? Surely, she has time to slip away and eat with us for a few hours."

Holiday looked down at the menu. Her hands were

shaking, and she wedged them beneath her legs. Okay, fine. Just because Daily wanted to play games didn't mean Holiday had to play them, too. She would do what she should've done on the phone the night before when Daily had called. She would ask Daily about the purpose of the weekend.

She jumped to her feet. "I'll be right back," she whispered to Jaxson. She scooted around her husband and darted out of the restaurant. Leonard was almost to the house, but she sprinted across the lawn and caught him just before he reached the back steps.

"No," she said, touching the innkeeper's arm to stop him.

Leonard stared back at her. "I beg your pardon, Mrs. Bridgewater?"

"I said no, as in no, you don't get to just drop a note off like that and walk away as if none of this concerns you."

Leonard narrowed his eyes. "I can't imagine what you're talking about."

She waved the note in his face. "Where is she? Where is Daily? She doesn't get to play with me like this."

Leonard took Holiday's hand in his. "I told her this was not a good idea."

"You told her? What does that mean?"

"Leaving," he said.

"Leaving?" Holiday looked around the inn's backyard. The sun had set, but the decorative lights behind the shrubs and along the side of the house created a relaxed, soothing ambiance for the grounds. It was the exact opposite of how she felt. "I don't understand. We all just got here."

Leonard looked around. "Come with me."

Holiday eyed the innkeeper and hesitated. He'd known more than he'd let on when they'd checked in that day.

Leonard gave her a tight smile and motioned again for her to follow, and she did.

Inside the house, she trailed Leonard through the parlor to the waiting elevator.

"Where are we going?" Holiday asked.

"Her last instructions to me were to let you into her room."

They entered the carriage, and when the elevator door opened on the third floor, he extended his hand for Holiday to exit first. She waited for him to show her the way, but he only took a few steps to Room 16.

Leonard opened the door and stood back as Holiday walked around the vacant room. The bed had been slept in, and used towels were on the floor. The shower was still wet, but there were no clothes in the armoire or bags on the chairs. Holiday opened the desk drawer and stopped. Inside was a gold triple-strand rope bracelet with five block letter charms attached.

D-A-I-L-Y.

"I suspect she's at the airport by now," Leonard said.

Daily was leaving Charleston. Was this what she'd meant when she'd told Beau she was ending this chapter of her life? Bring everyone to Wentworth Mansion, remind them what an awful friend Holiday had been, then vanish? She'd probably laughed all the way to CHS.

Holiday pulled out her phone and dialed Daily's number, but it went straight to voicemail. She stood by the window and redialed. Again, it went to voicemail, but this time she left a message.

"Daily, call me. What's going on?" She paused. What did she want to tell her? "Daily, I miss you."

Daily had called Holiday again and again that day,

twenty years ago. Holiday had never responded. Now, Daily was doing it to her.

"If that will be all, Mrs. Bridgewater…"

Leonard stepped back into the hallway, and Holiday followed.

They took the elevator back to the main floor. Leonard went to his desk, and Holiday slumped into one of his hard-back chairs. Leonard dropped the room key in his desk drawer, leaving it slightly ajar.

"Your weekend is still paid in full," he said. "Miss Southerleigh made sure of this before she left. Your dinners, any other massages you would like, and your room. She will cover all expenses."

One final dig to show how much better she was than Holiday.

Holiday looked up at the innkeeper. "May I ask you a question, Leonard?"

"By all means, ma'am."

"Were you here twenty years ago?"

Leonard shook his head. "I was not."

If Daily was gone, maybe Holiday didn't have to tell Jaxson what happened after all. He didn't need to know any more than the group. The whole ugly event could stay hidden. She just needed to return to dinner and spend the night. Tomorrow, they'd fly back to Dallas.

Leonard stood. "Ma'am, if there is nothing else, I will retire for the evening. It's been quite a busy day, as I'm sure it has been for you, too." He picked up his coat and hat. "If I may add one more thing, though. It was you, Mrs. Bridgewater, that Daily wanted here more than anyone else. She told me that herself. Well, goodnight."

Holiday nodded, stood, and walked to the giant ledger at

the front door. She watched as Leonard headed to the back door and left the house. She checked the ceilings. There were no cameras—none she could see anyway—and Leonard had forgotten to lock his desk.

She crossed her fingers, leaned over the desk, and lifted the key to Daily's room, just in case. Then she headed back to Circa 1886.

Everyone was in conversation and eating. They turned toward her as she scooted past Jaxson and slid back into her seat. Jaxson had ordered the cornmeal-crusted flounder and a romaine heart salad for her.

"You okay, baby?" he whispered. "Anything I can do?"

She forced a smile and kissed him on the cheek. "All good."

The food smelled amazing, and she suddenly realized how hungry she was.

Jaxson and Dave talked about golf. Payton and Beau talked about money. And Tú and Michael laughed at something Tú said. Michael reached for Tú's hand and squeezed it quickly before she pulled it back to her lap and smiled.

There was just one empty chair at the table. Daily had left before they'd even gotten started. It didn't make sense. It was unlike her to be so impulsive.

Daily was never impulsive. She always had a plan.

Twenty years ago, Holiday and Daily had planned to have dinner at Daily's favorite dive in uptown Dallas. However, they didn't have dinner that night because Holiday hadn't shown up at the last second.

No call. No apologies. Instead, she'd hopped a plane with Bobby Boudreaux and flown to Charleston.

To Wentworth Mansion. To Room 19.

And two nights later, Bobby was dead in the Grand Mansion Suite.

Daily had a plan, alright. She was doing to Holiday what Holiday had done to her.

Step by step, Daily was building a case against Holiday Trousseau Bridgewater.

A case for murder.

5

———————

"Isn't it just beautiful up here?" Jaxson asked.

It was chilly and windy outside the cupola, and Jaxson put his arm around his wife's waist and pulled her in. She snuggled into him, burrowing her shoulder into his chest. She felt good against him. And she smelled good, too.

Dinner had been a study in contrasts. After Daily's non-appearance, Jaxson couldn't help but notice a sudden change in the atmosphere around the table. The Crazy Eights started having fun. They were lighter and chattier once they'd learned their hostess was unavailable. Even Tú relaxed, and Jaxson decided it wasn't just the wine. They'd eaten. They'd laughed. They'd reminisced. And when it was over, they'd even hugged one another. It was as if they'd all suddenly exhaled simultaneously when they realized Daily Southerleigh wouldn't be joining them.

Holiday had been no different. From the moment he'd met her at the Charleston airport, she had been anxious and hypersensitive, avoiding his questions, gripping his hand, and constantly looking around to see who else might be nearby. He figured she was worried about her first meeting with Daily in two decades. It was only natural. Reunions like that are always awkward at first. But then she'd jumped up from the table with a violent start. And when she'd returned, a calmness had enveloped her, a relaxed pleasantness that drew the others in as she freely shared the funny and sometimes embarrassing moments of their first months of marriage. Holiday seemed to be enjoying herself for the first time since they'd arrived at Wentworth. He just hoped her lightheartedness would continue through the weekend. He made a note to talk to her about her feelings for Daily later that night. Getting her to talk about her emotions might help her maintain the joy he'd finally seen in her.

"Perhaps we should ask Leonard for sleeping bags and camp out under the stars," he said.

Holiday didn't say anything.

"You still thinking about Daily?" he asked, his chin resting on her head.

She nodded. "I'm trying not to. It's weird, you know? Gets us all here at the last second and then doesn't show up."

"Probably wasn't feeling well and just needed a moment to unwind. I'm sure it's a little nerve-racking seeing everyone again for the first time in two decades."

Holiday pulled away from Jaxson but took both of his hands in hers. "There's something I need to tell you. Daily is gone. She left."

Jaxson searched his wife's eyes for any hint that she was teasing. "She's not at the mansion?"

She shook her head. "Leonard took me to Daily's room. Her things are gone. But she left this." She pulled the gold triple-strand rope bracelet from her pocket.

Jaxson took the bracelet in his hands, fingering the small blocks of letters. The bracelet was well-worn with tiny scratches etched into the metal. But the silver clasp was newer, an obvious replacement at some point. "To skip dinner is one thing. But to leave the inn after getting everyone here? That's just bizarre. Did she say where she was going? A note? Anything?"

Holiday shook her head. "I tried calling several times but got sent to voicemail."

"Now we're all here for a weekend she planned without her."

She pulled him close. "I want to go home, Jax. This place gives me the creeps. All this talk about Bobby's murder, and now Daily leaves..."

Jaxson leaned in and kissed her. "You don't want to stay and have a wonderfully romantic weekend at Charleston's most glorious old inn? We'll take carriage rides through the old downtown and go out to Fort Sumter, where the first shots of the Civil War were fired."

Holiday gave him an eye. "Fort Sumter, dear? For real? That's your idea of a romantic weekend in Charleston?"

He gave her a sheepish grin and shrugged. "I don't know. I was thinking maybe we could salvage the weekend." He glanced at the spiral staircase inside the cupola. "Doesn't have to be Fort Sumter..."

She pursed her lips as she stared into the distance. "I just want to go home."

He let his eyes settle onto one of the white steeples lit up in the distance. The truth was, he wasn't ready to leave. The old inn would make an excellent setting for a novel, but he'd have to get to know it first, take photos, read up on its history, and talk to Leonard. If only he could get one more day...

"You do know Charleston is quite well known for its

restaurants. We'll skip Fort Sumter and eat our way down King Street and across Market."

Holiday looked up at him and kissed him lightly on the lips. "Let's go home. Tomorrow."

Jaxson smiled at her and nodded. Holiday pocketed Daily's bracelet and pulled Jaxson toward the cupola door. Inside, at the top of the spiraling staircase, he stopped and shone his phone's flashlight on the floor.

"I want to make sure there's no slippery goo up here again," he said. "The two of us tumbling down these stairs like Beau would be even less romantic than a visit to Fort Sumter."

Assured the area was clean, they headed back to their room. They took showers and snuggled into each other beneath the covers. Holiday lay on her left side, and Jaxson spooned up behind her, his naked body pressed into the back of hers. He snaked an arm around her waist and buried his face in her hair.

"You smell good," he said.

She turned her head back toward him. "You like spooning with me, don't you?"

"A lot."

Holiday turned her body around and pressed into him, their legs and feet entwined. "I can tell."

They made love, and an hour later, Jaxson turned off the table lamp on his side. They said their I love yous and their goodnights and drifted off.

Jaxson wasn't sure how long they'd been asleep, but a terrifying scream and a deadening thud woke him with a start, and he sat bolt upright in bed.

"What was that?" Holiday asked.

Jaxson jumped up and tossed on his robe as he headed for the door. "Stay here."

Outside their room, the grand staircase around the elevator was empty. He ran down the hall, where he found the body of a woman lying at the base of the spiral staircase, her long copper hair splayed out in a pool of blood. A leg and an arm twisted unnaturally behind her.

He reached two fingers to her neck. She was dead.

"Oh, my God," Holiday said in a half-whisper. "Daily."

Jaxson spun. Holiday had thrown on her robe and followed him.

She started to touch her friend, but Jaxson stopped her.

"No, baby. She's gone. There's nothing you can do." He looked up to the top of the stairs. Was the slimy goo up there again? "Stay here."

He stepped over Daily's body and took the spiral staircase two steps at a time. He didn't have his phone, but the moon's glow through the arched windows was just enough for Jaxson to see the clean floor. He stepped out on the wooden walkway. Nobody was there.

He gingerly made his way back down. Holiday stood over Daily's body, her hands to her face, sobbing softly. Tú stood behind her, her hands on Holiday's shoulders.

"Someone is trying to take out the Crazy Eights," Tú whispered to nobody.

Something a detective once told Jaxson popped into his head. *One death can mean one accident. Two accidents can only mean murder.*

"Will you take Holiday back to our room and wait with her until I return?" Jaxson asked Tú.

She nodded and walked Holiday down the hall.

Jaxson lit off down the grand staircase and found Geoffrey sitting at Leonard's desk.

"Someone's dead," Jaxson said. "Call the police."

Half an hour later, Leonard, four paramedics, and a man who'd identified himself as Detective Bonetti were beside Jaxson at the bottom of the spiral staircase. Bonetti was a short, rotund man with gray hair that touched his shoulders and a full gray beard that brushed his chest. He wore thick black glasses, and each time he asked Jaxson or Leonard a question, his only response to the answer was a crisp humph. The coroner arrived shortly after.

After several hours of collecting evidence, Bonetti and the coroner ascertained that Daily's fall and subsequent death were likely accidental, perhaps even due to alcohol impairment and an inability to navigate the narrow, spiraling stairs. The coroner took Daily's body down the grand staircase, and Jaxson and Bonetti followed, the detective assuring Jaxson that an autopsy would be conducted to rule on the manner and cause of death officially. The area surrounding the spiral staircase was taped off until the inn could arrange for a biohazard cleaning crew to visit the mansion the following day.

Jaxson waited until the authorities had left, then took the grand staircase to the fourth floor. Tú sat quietly before the lit fireplace when he entered their room. Holiday was asleep in bed.

He nodded to Tú. "Thanks for staying with her."

"It was no problem," Tú whispered. "I gave her a sleeping pill, and that knocked her right out."

"A sleeping pill?" A flash of alarm struck Jaxson. He'd only met Tú a few hours earlier, and Holiday hadn't seen her in twenty years. A stranger had drugged his wife. "Does she know you gave her a pill?"

Tú shrugged it off. "I think so, but she was pretty out of it. She'll be fine."

She gave him a wave of her pinkie and let herself out.

It incensed Jaxson that Tú would drug his wife. Holiday hadn't been in the right frame of mind to consent.

Three people had fallen or almost fallen down those spiraling steps in one day. Were they being targeted?

Maybe Beau would know of someone who might want to harm them.

Jaxson ran down the grand staircase to the main floor. It was almost 3:00 a.m. It would not be easy for Beau to come to the door, but he would want to know about Daily anyway.

Beau eventually opened the door, wearing his robe and a black orthopedic boot. As one might expect, his hair was a mess.

"I have some bad news, Beau," Jaxson began, and explained about Daily.

"That's just awful." Beau sat on the edge of the bed. "Someone should do something before this inn gets hit with a lawsuit. That's three of us in one day."

"Can you think of anyone who'd want to harm the Crazy Eights?" Jaxson asked. "Did you guys ever kick someone out of the group or, I don't know, piss someone off?"

Beau rubbed his eyes. "I can't think of anyone. And honestly, that would be a long time to hold a grudge. Twenty years?"

Jaxson nodded. "It's just...it's just too much of a coincidence. You know?" He let out a breath. "Do you think it's possible someone in the group would do something like this?"

"One of the Crazy Eights?" Beau guffawed. "Daily gets us all here, so one of us decided to take everyone out?" He shook his head. "That'd be pretty easy to figure out. The last man standing is the killer."

"I suppose." Jaxson flashed back to that old Agatha Christie novel, where everyone gets invited to an island, and one by one, they all end up murdered. "Maybe it was somebody's plan twenty years ago to take you all out, someone from outside the group, and they started with Bobby, but they didn't get a chance to finish, and now that you're back, they've started up again."

Beau winced. "Like a serial killer? What would they have been doing all these years in between? Killing other people, or just waiting for a chance to kill the rest of us, hoping we'd all get back together at the same place on the same day?" He shook his head. "Honestly, it makes more sense that three of us had a terrible accident on those winding stairs today, and a fatal accident for one of us."

Jaxson drew in a deep breath and let it out slowly. "Yeah, okay. I was just wondering." He thanked Beau for his time and promised to catch up the next day.

He was standing outside his room again when he decided to take another trip to the cupola.

Finding Daily's body had been surreal, dream-like, and he needed to see once more where she had fallen, almost as if to prove to himself that the tragedy really had occurred. Death had always been like that with him, difficult to believe unless he could touch it.

His stepfather had died in his sleep when Jaxson was ten. At the funeral, during the viewing, Jaxson had stood on tiptoes to get a better view of the man who'd raised him and slipped a finger over the edge of the casket to see if it was real, if Jim Bridgewater truly was dead. Jaxson knew he was when he touched his stepdad's cold hand. It was then that reality had settled over little Jaxson. Jim Bridgewater would not be coming home or having dinner, and would never again take Jaxson to the park or a Cowboys football game. Touching the old man's cold, lifeless body had settled the matter.

But Daily's lifeless body had not been cold. Her neck, when he'd felt for a pulse, and her hand were still warm, as though just a minute earlier she'd been as alive as he and Holiday. In an instant, she was gone. What had she even been doing up there? Hadn't she gone to the airport? She'd gotten her old friends together for the weekend, abandoned them at dinner, and then been found dead at the bottom of the spiral staircase. Touching Daily's warm, lifeless body had settled nothing for Jaxson.

He slipped beneath the "Do Not Enter" tape around the bottom of the spiral staircase and headed to the top. The floor was still dry and clean, just as he thought it had been.

He stepped out on the deck and studied sleepy old downtown Charleston in the cool morning. In a few hours, the streets would be bustling again, and everyone would be unaware that a death had occurred right where they lived.

Not a death. A murder.

It had to be murder. It was the only thing that made sense, even if the reason for it didn't.

Tú was right. It was as if, one by one, someone was trying to kill off each member of the Crazy Eights.

It was almost as if Bobby's ghost had come back to take revenge on the twentieth anniversary of his murder.

Holiday woke with a start at 4:43 am, suddenly remembering Daily's lifeless body lying on the floor down the hall from their room. Her heart ached, and she cried silently into her pillow.

Jaxson was snoring next to her. How late had he been up? Hadn't Tú been with her for a while?

The moon's glow slipped through the cracks between the plantation shutters. The key to Daily's room sat on the dresser beside the bed. Daily hadn't left when she'd told Leonard she had. Or she'd come back. Had she been on the property, hiding, when Leonard had taken Holiday to Daily's room? Maybe she'd returned to the room after Holiday and Leonard had gone downstairs. Would she have noticed that the bracelet was gone? She could've left other items in the room when she came back. One quick trip to her room while everyone was asleep would satisfy Holiday's mind.

She picked up the key and her phone and slipped quietly from the bed. She wrapped her robe around her, tiptoed to the door, and slipped into the hallway. She took the grand staircase to the third floor and stood before Daily's room. It would be spooky going in there while it was dark out, especially now that her friend was dead.

She let herself in and flipped the light switch. She half-expected to see Daily waiting for her, saying it had all been just one big joke. But she wasn't there. The bed was still unmade. There were still no toiletries in the bathroom. The room was exactly as it had been at dinner.

If only she could talk to Daily again and tell her how sorry she was for everything that had happened. She should've gone to dinner with Daily that night, twenty years ago. If she had, she wouldn't be standing in the room of her dead friend.

They'd had a game when they were growing up. Whenever they visited each other, they would sneak into the bathroom, turn on the hot shower, and steam up the mirror to write a note to the other. When the steam disappeared, so did the message. It was only later in the evening, when they took showers, that the invisible messages would reappear. It was their secret way to remind each other they were always there, even when they weren't.

The last message Daily had left on Holiday's mirror was the night before that dinner they were supposed to have, the night before Holiday ran off to Charleston with Bobby. Daily had left just five words on her mirror.

I will love you always.

Then, Holiday ghosted her and snuck away with Daily's ex-fiancé, and the messages ended.

Holiday studied herself in the bathroom mirror. Her face was lined from the crinkles in the pillow. Her hair was a tangled mess. Her eyes were bloodshot, and more tears threatened to spill over her cheeks.

In the mirror, she saw the reflection of the shower behind her. She opened the glass door and turned on the hot water. Then, she sat on the tub's edge to wait until the mirror was fogged. She would write Daily one last note. One more secret message. And this time, she would tell her she was sorry.

It took about ten minutes to get the bathroom hot and steamy. She stood to write her apology, but three-inch-tall words stared back at her.

I still love you always.
Replay the day.

Tears ran down Holiday's cheeks, and she swiped at her eyes to see the words better.

Daily had still loved her after all these years.

"Oh, I love you, too, sweet friend!" she said. "And I've missed you!"

Guilt and shame overwhelmed her as she remembered the selfish pride that had kept her from calling Daily and telling her those words for years. All that time, she had loved Daily, and she had missed her terribly. Why hadn't she told her?

Replay the day? What was she telling her to do?

And there was something else. Below the message was a backward checkmark. What did it mean?

Holiday took her phone from her robe and snapped a picture of the message. Once the steam was gone, her friend's final secret note would be, too.

She sat on the side of the tub for a long time until the hot water ran out, the steam disappeared, and the message faded away. Then, she turned off the shower, turned off the lights, and headed back upstairs.

Holiday stopped at the top of the grand staircase.

Replay the day. That's what Daily had been doing. And it's what she'd been making Holiday do.

Daily wasn't building a case against Holiday. She had been walking her through the case again, helping Holiday see what she had already discovered.

Daily had uncovered the identity of Bobby's killer.

She'd known it wasn't Holiday. At least, technically, it wasn't.

But before Daily had gotten too far, before she'd been able to reveal the truth, she'd been killed.

Bobby's murderer had stopped her before she had

stopped him. That meant Bobby's murderer was back at Wentworth Mansion.

And now he'd killed Daily.

Holiday opened the door to their room, dropped her robe to the floor, and slipped into bed next to Jaxson. She scooched up behind him, pressing against his bare back, her arm wrapping around his chest.

He stirred softly and mumbled. "Where did you go, love?"

She kissed him on the back of his neck. "Daily's room. She left me a message."

Jaxson rolled over and propped his head up. "A message?"

Holiday nodded. "'Replay the day.' That's what it said."

"What does that mean?"

She kissed him on the lips. "It means we are going to find out who killed Bobby Boudreaux and Daily Southerleigh."

6

Holiday reached for her husband's hand as they took the steps of the grand staircase down to the main floor. Daily's final secret message had changed everything. If she and Jaxson were to find Bobby and Daily's murderer, she would have to come clean with Jaxson and reveal a secret she'd not told anyone in twenty years. She'd have to do what her mother had been incapable of: tell the truth.

Her steps felt lighter this morning, but her stomach was still knotted. Once she told Jaxson, there'd be no going back. Her past would be his, too, and it might not be something he'd bargained for when they married.

"Good morning, Mr. and Mrs. Bridgewater," Leonard said as they entered the foyer. His face was drawn, his voice solemn and low.

"Just the man we were coming to see," Holiday said. "Are you...okay?"

Leonard slumped behind his desk, his elbows on the blotter, rubbing both temples. Holiday sat in one of his chairs and smoothed out her gray and pink printed wrap dress. Jaxson stood beside her.

The innkeeper pressed his lips and shook a drooping head. "The owners of Wentworth want answers, and they want them from me. First, there was the goo where Mr. Culverhouse fell. We cleaned it up, and I have assured the owners that it wasn't there when Miss Southerleigh fell. Of course, there is the possibility of lawsuits. Thankfully, Mr. Culverhouse only had a hairline fracture, as I understand, and he has been so good-natured about it and has dismissed any notion of legal action. Still, we are quite concerned with what Miss Southerleigh's family will say. A highly reputable woman like her falling at our establishment…" He let out a deep sigh and shook his head. "She checked out hours before and said she was going to the airport. What was she even doing here?"

Leonard hadn't known Daily's plans after all. There had been no conspiracy between the two. Holiday placed a hand on Leonard's arm. "Perhaps we can help."

Leonard raised his head.

"Daily didn't bring us together like this just for a college reunion." She glanced at Jaxson. "We believe her death wasn't accidental and has ties to another death that occurred here some twenty years ago."

"Mr. Bobby Boudreaux," Leonard said.

"You know of it?" Jaxson asked.

Leonard nodded. "Everyone who works here is trained on the mansion's history, even the more unsavory pieces of the inn's story. You're not suggesting more foul play, I hope."

Holiday lowered her voice. "That's exactly what we're saying. The first death is tied to the second."

Leonard leaned over his desk. "Please don't tell me you think a killer has checked into Wentworth Mansion."

"We want to investigate what happened," Holiday said, "but we need your help. We want to gather everyone in the conference room downstairs, just as Daily was planning, to go through whatever it is she dug up."

"But there's nothing down there," Leonard said. "I checked this morning."

Jaxson cocked his head. "I thought she had some material for us to go over."

"That's what she told me." Leonard shook his head. "I simply can't believe Miss Southerleigh is gone. She came to the inn often, sometimes only to say hello. We held exhibitions for her artwork here. Of course, she and I talked about the night Mr. Boudreaux was killed. She often would say to me, 'Leonard, if we want to catch a killer, we shouldn't think like the murderer but like his victim.' She was always trying to see the murder from Mr. Boudreaux's viewpoint. Such a sweet woman. Who would want to harm her?"

"That's what we're going to find out," Holiday said. "Would you contact everyone in our group and let them know that we are meeting in the downstairs conference room at ten o'clock?"

Leonard nodded. "Yes, of course."

Jaxson took her hand. "We should get some breakfast before it shuts down."

Holiday nodded, but she didn't think she could eat. Did Jaxson really need to know she'd been in the Grand Mansion Suite when Bobby died? She could feel her shoulders sagging as they walked across the lawn to the restaurant.

Halfway across the yard, Jaxson stopped to pluck a small, clear box from the hearty blades of the St. Augustine grass.

"I'd been wondering where you were," he said.

"What did you find, dear?"

He held out a box of yellow Sprite Tic Tacs. "Whoever

was at the bottom of the staircase yesterday must've taken this. Now I find it in the backyard. This little box is getting around. I wonder if the person who took it realizes he lost it."

He pocketed the mints and held the door open to Circa 1886. They stopped short after they passed through the bar. At the same long table where they'd eaten the night before, the other Crazy Eights sat in their same seats. Tú was no longer wearing the bucket hat. She'd tied her hair back in a high pony but still wore her sunglasses and N95 mask. Michael sat in a blue plaid western button-down shirt and blue jeans, his arms crossed, nodding at Tú, who stopped talking when she saw Jaxson and Holiday. In a black tee and shorts, Beau rested his arm through the handpiece of one of his crutches as he broke a golden-brown croissant into bite-size pieces, popping one into his mouth. He smiled, pointed to a plate piled high with pastries, and waved the couple over. And Dave and Payton, in matching pink golf shirts and leaning toward each other in a hushed conversation, quickly straightened as Jaxson and Holiday approached.

A flash of heat enveloped Holiday as she and Jaxson filed past the group and took their places on the table's far end. Every eye at the table followed the pair to their chairs. "We all had the same idea about an early morning break-fast." Her voice was weak and unconvincing.

Michael forced a smile. "We've just had a little meeting, and I'm afraid you've been elected."

Holiday unrolled her napkin. "I don't understand."

"The question arose as to whether we should continue with our reunion weekend or cancel it altogether," Dave said.

"And?" Jaxson propped his elbows on the table.

"We decided to continue," Tú said.

Beau's crutch fell on Michael, who shook his head and pushed it back toward its owner. "Under one condition." Beau winked. "That you take the lead with whatever Daily wanted us to do."

Michael rubbed his hands together. "We want you to continue her investigation into Bobby's murder."

Holiday stared at Michael, her eyes wide.

"Please don't tell us you thought this was an actual college reunion." Tú extended her hands toward everyone. "Let's face it, most of us haven't spoken to each other in almost two decades. Daily turned her back on us after Bobby's death. But then, suddenly, she gets her hair on fire, and we all have to be here?" She scoffed. "Honestly. The woman was just too much."

Holiday felt Jaxson looking at her. He had to have so many questions, and she'd let too many opportunities go by without explaining things. She could feel her stomach turning again.

"Why Holiday?" Jaxson asked. "Why don't one of you finish what Daily started?"

"We're not talking about Holiday." Michael pointed at Jaxson. "We want you to take the case." A slight smile brushed his face. "She's one of us—a Crazy Eight. You're the outsider. You're the one with a more objective perspective."

Tú ripped the napkin from her lap and threw it on the table. "We want you to find the killer of Bobby Boudreaux and Daily Southerleigh!" She lowered her voice, her eyes cutting to each face. "The killer is among us."

Jaxson lowered his chin and squinted at the group before them. "What makes you think the two deaths are connected?"

"Stands to reason, doesn't it?" Michael put an arm on Tú's shoulder. "Daily's lifelong ambition was to find Bobby's killer. Suddenly, we all get a call to come here immediately, that she has some big news to tell us, in the same place where he was killed. But before she can tell us, she's dead."

"The killer murdered her before she could point him out," said Dave.

"Someone at this table." Payton's voice came out small and fearful, just above a whisper.

Holiday looked around the room and found Tú staring at her. She diverted her eyes back to Jaxson, her hands clenched tightly in her lap.

Jaxson shrugged. "Why couldn't it be—?

"Someone from the outside? Two different killers? A coincidence?" Michael shook his head. "Not a chance. Payton's right. It's somebody at this table."

"It had to be one of us," Beau said.

"Why not just let the police lead the investigation?" Jaxson asked. "Turn over everything Daily had to the authorities."

"No!" Tú snapped, crossing her arms.

Michael smiled at Tú. "We can't...Rather, I should say, we don't want to do that. Every one of us has something personal to hide, and we'd rather keep it that way." He gave Jaxson a stern look. "Including your wife."

Everyone nodded and looked at Holiday.

Holiday stared at Michael, holding her breath.

Beau raised himself with his crutches. "You'd be doing us a huge favor. One of our own has now killed two of our own. We need answers."

Michael stood next to Beau. "Well, what's it going to be?"

Holiday watched her husband consider the offer. If he agreed, talking to everyone and asking questions would be easier. They would be permitted to investigate the group. On the other hand, they weren't asking her to investigate, only

Jaxson, which meant the eye of suspicion was still on her just as much as it was on the others. Maybe that was the point. Perhaps they thought she killed Bobby and Daily, and they had elected Jaxson to do the dirty work of proving her guilty, just as she had brought him on the trip to prove her innocence.

Jaxson's words were measured. "Yes. I suppose I will. If you want me to."

"Then it's settled," Dave said. "Just tell us what you need."

Jaxson looked around the table. "I guess I'll need to talk to everyone."

"You'll need to get started straight away," said Michael. "We're all checking out by eleven tomorrow morning. You have just over twenty-four hours."

Jaxson nodded, and the group disbanded, leaving only Jaxson and Holiday behind.

He turned to her. "Did you put them up to that?"

Another pain of guilt shot through her stomach. Use her husband to manipulate the group in her favor? She shook her head. "No, but I'm not surprised. It's like Michael said. You're the outsider. Which means, dear, I'm one of your suspects."

"You're not a suspect. You're my wife."

"Trust me, I'd rather just be your wife, but in this case, I'm afraid Michael is correct." She lowered her eyes to the breakfast menu. "They all think I killed Daily."

"That's crazy."

She bit her lower lip and stared into the distance, willing herself not to tear up. "Because they all think I killed Bobby."

He narrowed his eyes at her and blinked. "What do you mean?"

The waitress approached the table. "Hello, folks. Looks like you guys are the last two standing." She pulled out her flip pad and a pencil. "What beverages can I get you?"

Jaxson's eyes were on Holiday. "Two Diet Cokes."

"For breakfast?" The waitress snickered, then caught herself. "Perfect. I'll get those started and let you look at the menu."

Holiday looked away. Her chest felt heavy. The words were out there now. Wasn't the truth supposed to set her free? All she wanted to do was curl up in a ball and disappear.

Jaxson placed a finger beneath her chin and brought her back toward him. "Let's start at the beginning, love. Tell me about when you came here twenty years ago, how you stayed in Room 19, and how you ended up in the Grand Mansion Suite with Bobby when he died."

Holiday's eyes widened. "But...how did...?"

Her husband patted her hand. "I'll tell you how I knew, and then you tell me everything that happened."

<hr>

About a year before Jaxson met Holiday, he'd interviewed an Austin detective who'd noted that murder suspects often get less interested in the deceased and more interested in deception the longer they're under suspicion. It aptly described what he and Holiday had witnessed at the breakfast table. Not one tear had been shed for the Crazy Eight member who'd brought them all to the inn and had been murdered looking for a killer.

Holiday took several bites of a bagel piled high with cream cheese.

"Would you like some bagel to go with that cream cheese, lover?" Jaxson asked.

Holiday licked her lips and smirked at him. "Okay, Mr. Smarty Pants, how long have you known?"

"That you'd been to Room 19 at Wentworth Mansion and been the prime suspect in the murder of Bobby Boudreaux?" He checked his watch. "Going on about nineteen hours."

She took another bite of the bagel. "What tipped you off?"

"Well, let's see. First, it was the fact that even though Geoffrey never told us about the fridge in the antique armoire, you just went right to it and pulled out a couple of Diet Cokes, like you'd been in that room before."

"Could've been a lucky guess."

He bit into his bagel. "I've been in plenty of hotels, and that's the last place I'd suspect a fridge."

"Okay. Point in your favor. What else?"

"You also turned on the gas in our fireplace with the switch behind the curtain. You already knew it was there."

"Fine," she admitted. "Another point for you. What else?"

"When I overheard the argument at the bottom of the cupola, a woman mentioned that several people here were in the same room as last time, which only confirmed what I suspected."

Holiday scrunched up her nose. "I wonder who was arguing? It can't be the Crazy Eights. Only Bobby and I were here that weekend. Well, sort of. But she came later. Of course, if one of them killed him, that can't be true." Holiday added more cream cheese to her bagel. "What about knowing I was the prime suspect in Bobby's murder?"

"That one took a little more deduction. I figured if you

weren't going to tell me you'd been here before, it must be for a pretty good reason. Daily had gotten us all the way here to figure out Bobby's murder, and she wanted us where it all went down. Then there was the fact that Bobby dumped Daily, a woman he was engaged to, only to travel to Charleston, one of the most romantic cities in the United States. And I had to ask myself, what would cause a man to do that, and what would cause two lifelong friends to never speak to each other for decades?"

Holiday rolled her eyes. "You just think you're so smart, don't you?"

"And the answer to those two questions is the same. Bobby had dumped Daily and run away with you. And if you had come here with Bobby, and then he died or, better yet, was murdered, that would automatically make you the number one suspect. So, I had to ask myself, why didn't you mention this? Even you would've told me if you'd been charged and gone to trial."

"Thank you for that ringing endorsement, dear."

"Something happened that made the police think otherwise about you." He popped the final piece of bagel in his mouth. "Somebody gave you an alibi."

Holiday crossed her arms and smiled. "That was very good, Sherlock."

Jaxson waved her off. "Elementary, my dear wife." He wiped the crumbs from her lips and kissed her.

She frowned. "I'm sorry, Jaxson."

He reached for her hand. "For what, baby? You didn't do anything wrong."

"For not telling you straight away. I wanted you with me to convince Daily that I didn't kill Bobby, even though I kinda helped without knowing it."

Jaxson pulled his chair closer to hers. "Six months of

marriage isn't that long. We're still figuring out how to trust each other. I would've probably done the same thing."

She leaned forward and kissed him. "I love you so much. And truly, thank you for being with me. I need you now more than ever."

"That's what husbands are for. But now I need to know your side of the story. What happened that weekend when you and Bobby came to Wentworth?"

Holiday gave him a sideways frown. "Are you sure you can trust me, knowing I was a suspect in a man's murder? Who's to say I didn't kill Daily to stop her from revealing my true identity?"

He waggled a finger at her. "Whoever murdered Daily likely murdered Bobby too, and I know you didn't murder Daily because your sweet, naked body was scooched up next to mine when it happened." He winked. "I think I can still trust you."

"What can I get you both for breakfast?"

Jaxson and Holiday looked up at the waitress, her pad in her hand.

"I'll just have some pancakes and grits." Jaxson turned to his wife.

"I'll have what he's having."

"Very well." The waitress turned toward the kitchen, and Jaxson turned toward his wife.

"Okay, *killer*, time to tell your story."

7

"I wasn't supposed to be here."

Holiday's voice was soft, and her head swam as she struggled for where to begin the story of her first visit to Wentworth Mansion. Relating that trip would be embarrassing, and that's what would make it hard. She'd been a fool that weekend. But equally difficult would be not knowing how Jaxson would respond. Would he understand she was no longer the same young woman she'd been all those years ago? Or would he be more like her father?

"Holi," her mother once said holding both of Holiday's hands, "when you marry a man like Marcus Emilian Trousseau, or when that man is your father, and he has had a particularly troublesome day, it is better for everyone to leave him out of anything unrelated to the business." Her mother's hands had been like talons on Holiday's. "Don't ever worry your father."

And Holiday hadn't.

But were all men like this?

Holiday checked Jaxson for any signs of disappointment,

70

but he only offered a gentle, coaxing smile. She clasped her hands to keep them from trembling.

"The day Bobby died?" Jaxson asked.

"That whole weekend. I was so jealous of them."

"Bobby and Daily?"

She nodded. "From the moment they started dating. He'd been in our group for about three months, and I was instantly attracted to him. I'd kept waiting for him to make a move. But then he fell for Daily, and I...I mean, it just hit me hard, you know?"

Jaxson watched her, his blue eyes earnest, waiting for her to finish. He smiled again and nodded, and she relaxed her shoulders, feeling the tension drain a little. Jaxson wasn't like her father.

"He and I had always flirted," she continued, "and I don't know...when he began asking Daily out, I thought maybe he was teasing me, letting me know he was some highly sought-after commodity."

"Did Daily know how you felt?"

Holiday shook her head. "I think she was too much in love to know what anyone around her was doing. That's just the way it is." She reached for Jaxson's hand. "It was that way with us, right?"

"Absolutely." Jaxson sat up straighter in his chair. "So, Daily and Bobby are dating, and..."

Holiday took in another deep breath. "Then they got engaged. It was so fast, within weeks. I don't know whose idea it was, but suddenly, Daily had a ring on her finger and was making wedding plans. One hundred days. That's how long their engagement was supposed to be."

The waitress approached the table with their plates, and Holiday paused her story.

"If you two need anything," said the waitress, her hands on her hips, "let me know."

Jaxson thanked her and turned back to Holiday. "One hundred days is not very long."

Holiday cut into her stack of pancakes. "All eight of us had just graduated five months earlier. We had known things would be different after graduation, but we made a pact to stay in touch, no matter what happened. That wasn't going to be a problem for Dave and Payton. Those two were already married. But then, suddenly, Daily and Bobby are engaged."

"And here you are, fresh out of college, with no plans for life, and the man you've been attracted to is suddenly marrying your best friend."

"I felt so lost and behind. And then, out of nowhere, with the wedding only a couple of weeks away, Bobby says he has something important to tell me. We meet at my apartment and he says he can't marry Daily. He doesn't want to hurt her, but at the same time, he says he can't spend the rest of his life with her, and it's killing him."

Jaxson took a sip of soda. "Did he tell you why?"

Holiday could feel the heat rising in her face. Her heart beat wildly, and she resisted the urge to put a hand to her chest. "He said he loved me and always had since we met and couldn't imagine life without me."

"Wow."

"That's what I said! I asked him if he'd told Daily, and he said he'd just broken up with her. He said he needed time to clear his mind and wanted to go to Charleston."

"And he wanted you to come with him."

Holiday set down her fork and knife. "I was floored. When he came over, I thought it might be his final goodbye. The next thing I knew, he said he wanted us to begin dating and asked me to go to a beautiful old mansion for the most romantic weekend ever."

"I can see how that would be hard to pass up."

"I immediately said yes, but I had this huge surge of guilt. Here I was about to have this amazing weekend with the ex-fiancé of my lifelong best friend. And so, I did what every terrible best friend would do. I said yes to Bobby and avoided every call Daily made that weekend. She must've called me twenty times to talk about what had happened. I was the one she would turn to for that. But what was I supposed to do? Take her call and pretend I wasn't with the love of her life? By the end of the second day, the phone calls stopped, and I never heard from her again until the day before yesterday."

Jaxson laid his napkin on the table. "What happened after you and Bobby got to the mansion?"

"We checked into Room 19. We had dinner right here in one of those booths by the wall. And the next day, we went on a carriage ride and took the ferry to Fort Sumter."

He gave her a look. "Dang, I wanted to go there with you. I thought you said that wouldn't be romantic."

"Sorry, dear." She gave him a sheepish grin and patted his hand. Why did every man want to see old forts? "I would love to go there with you, but it's still not very romantic."

"Okay, back to what happened..."

"That night, after a day of sightseeing, something told me the weekend was all wrong. I felt like I'd been some silly schoolgirl caught up in a fairy tale. I realized I was losing my best friend. I told him we needed separate rooms and more time to think this over. Truthfully, though, that day of looking around Charleston was enough for me to know Bobby wasn't the man I wanted to spend the rest of my life with."

"Why?"

"I saw a different side of him. He was pretentious. He spent a lot of time talking about himself. He said he had a big business opportunity here but wouldn't tell me what it was. Not once did he ask about me. It was as if he already knew all he wanted." She lowered her voice and channeled Bobby. "Nothing left to discover here!"

Jaxson laughed at her theatrics.

Holiday let out a little laugh, but the tears were starting to form in the corner of her eyes, and she quickly dabbed at them with her napkin. "Thank you for listening to my stupid story."

"It's not stupid. Go on."

Holiday sat up straighter and cleared her throat. "We were sitting in the mansion's library. Bobby was flipping through a deck of cards while I told him how I felt. I could tell he was annoyed, but he wasn't rude. I had to go to the restroom, and when I got back, Bobby was talking with the innkeeper, who offered to put him in the Grand Mansion Suite. Later that night, he called me to say he needed to see me. Asked if I could come to his room."

"And you went?"

Holiday opened her mouth, but was cut off by a voice from the bar.

"Excuse me, Mr. and Mrs. Bridgewater?"

The couple turned to see Leonard approaching their table.

"Oh, Leonard," said Holiday, "that reminds me, there's no need to gather everyone together for a meeting at ten."

"Very well." Leonard nodded and handed Holiday a tiny envelope with her name in beautiful script. "I'm sorry to intrude on your wonderful breakfast, but I was asked to deliver this to you."

"Who's it from?" Jaxson asked.

"I believe Mrs. Bridgewater will find the answer inside," Leonard said. "If there is nothing more?"

Holiday shook her head and studied the envelope as Leonard walked away. She then removed a small notecard from the envelope.

"Meet me in the library at ten o'clock," Holiday read. "Judith Rainier, Room 9." She looked up at Jaxson. "Who is Judith Rainier?"

Jaxson pulled out his phone and shook his head. "No one like her comes up on Google. Maybe I should go with you to this meeting."

Jaxson had a point. Still, the envelope had been addressed only to her, and if this Judith knew something about Daily's murder, she might not be so willing to share if Holiday brought someone else along. Plus, they'd be in the mansion's library around the corner from Leonard. "It'll be okay. We'll be safe."

He gave her a look. "A lot of dead bodies show up in libraries."

Holiday let out a nervous laugh. "Only in mysteries, dear. I'll be fine, and when it's over, I'll let you know all about it."

"I still don't like it, but let's finish your story. You said Bobby called you and asked you to come to his room. And I'm gathering you went?"

Holiday sighed. "I wasn't quite as worldly-wise as I am now. I didn't want to, but I went to meet him anyway, and he asked me if I would join him for a drink. He said he felt lonely and realized he'd messed things up with Daily. He said he would call her as soon as he returned to Dallas. He didn't want her to know where he was."

Jaxson raised a hand. "Where were you two at this point?"

"We were sitting in that front room in the Grand Mansion Suite, the living area, where Leonard said the men used to smoke."

Jaxson nodded.

"He had a bottle of wine sitting between us on the antique table and a few glasses. He said it was a gift from the hotel, accompanied by a note thanking him for his visit. He poured a glass for each of us, handed one to me, and we both began to drink and talk, mainly about the day."

Holiday paused. She fumbled for a reason to skip over this next part of the story. She'd never told anyone what she did that night. But if she couldn't trust her new husband...

"And?"

"And then he wanted me to go to bed with him." She looked at her hands in her lap. "I thought, 'Why did you come down here, stupid?' And he was insistent, almost like I owed him. He kept reminding me of all he'd done for me that weekend. So I did something I shouldn't have done." She took a drink of her soda.

"You didn't kill him, did you?"

Holiday almost choked. "No! At least, I don't think so."

"You don't remember?"

"Bobby was insistent. He even started touching me. So, I kept pouring him wine, putting him off, hoping he'd get so drunk that he'd fall asleep, and I could slip out of the room without marring our friendship."

"That was your plan, to ply him with alcohol so he'd pass out?"

"Well..." Holiday grimaced. "Yeah, I guess it was."

"Okay, go on, what happened next?"

She shrugged. "Then I fell asleep."

"You fell asleep?"

She nodded. "One moment, I'm sipping wine, pouring glass after glass for Bobby, and the next thing I know, I wake up in a chair. Almost two hours had gone by. I had a throbbing headache, and I wondered if I'd been drugged. But then I thought, no, Bobby wouldn't have done that. And he drank from the same bottle. I looked around for Bobby, but he wasn't in the chair like he had been earlier."

"Where was he?"

"He was in bed, and I thought he was asleep. I started feeling bad about over-serving him, so I shook him to see if he was okay, but he didn't budge. I felt his neck, and there was no pulse. And I remember thinking, 'Oh, God, what have I done?' I pulled out my phone—it was one of those old flip kinds back then—and I called the first person I could think of."

"Your dad?" Jaxson asked.

Holiday shook her head. "Tú."

"Tú? Why her?"

"She was already in law school, and I don't know, I just figured I could trust her."

"Didn't your dad have some kind of legal team you could've turned to?"

"That would've been the right thing to do, but Daddy didn't even know I was there, and he didn't like Bobby anyway. I just wanted to keep the whole thing off the radar. Anyway, Tú told me she was an hour away. She was in Rock Hill visiting her grandmother. She told me to go straight to my room and not leave."

"Tú was your alibi."

Holiday nodded. "When she got here, I told her everything. Well, almost everything. I didn't tell her how I kept pushing more and more wine on Bobby. It was about three in the morning, and she said we needed to go back to Bobby's room to wipe it down. There should be no trace of me in that room. We took the elevator to the main floor and prayed we wouldn't be seen. Nobody was at the front desk, and Tú went to the door of his room and opened it."

"It wasn't locked?"

Holiday shook her head. "It wasn't locked when I went to see him either. Anyway, the two of us slipped inside. Oh, my God, it was so creepy going back in that room. I couldn't look at Bobby. Everything was so surreal. It was like watching a movie, only I was in it. We wiped everything down and then returned to Room 19."

"Including the bottle and the glasses? You wiped them down, too?"

Holiday bit her lip. "When I went back in there, they were gone. Someone had taken them. The killer, I guess."

Jaxson shook his head. "That doesn't make sense. Why would the killer bother to knock the two of you out, kill him, leave you alone, then take the very evidence that could've incriminated you?"

Holiday stopped and stared out of the restaurant window. Outside, a couple was looking at the entrance to Circa 1886. The woman checked her watch, glanced at the restaurant, and continued.

"And when the police questioned you, Tú was your alibi? She said you'd been together all evening?"

Holiday nodded again, realizing she missed the person Tú had been in college. Kind. Giving. Understanding. Tú hadn't come across as any of those things at dinner the previous night.

Jaxson rubbed his forehead. "I don't know. That's not making sense. What about the innkeeper on duty? Didn't they ask him about Tú? He would have some idea that Tú hadn't checked into the inn and would know she wasn't there when you and Bobby asked him for the Grand Mansion Suite. What about the cell phone records?"

"I hate to say it, but we lied to the police. We told them we had been together since dinner, and neither of us had seen Bobby." Holiday shrugged. "They believed us and didn't question further."

"What was the cause and manner of death?" Jaxson asked. "Did you ever find out?"

"Someone had injected him with a mixture of tramadol and sertraline, and, I guess, with the wine, the combination killed him." Holiday swallowed hard. "If I hadn't pushed so much wine on Bobby, he might still be alive today. Maybe he could've fought back."

"Are you saying that while you were knocked out, someone else entered and forced him to take powerful narcotics? Why would he even do that?"

"He wouldn't. The autopsy reported that Bobby had a high dose of midazolam in his system. I'm guessing we both did. That's what knocked us out. And while I was asleep, someone came in, stuck a needle in his neck, and administered a large dose of tramadol and sertraline straight into his veins. He probably died instantly."

"And the needle?"

"They never found it. All they found was the puncture wound."

"And you never heard anything?"

"Knocked out until I woke up and realized what had happened." She sighed. "I'm partly to blame for Bobby's death."

Jaxson shook his head. "No. Whoever wanted him dead knocked you both out, then killed him."

"How are you two doing?"

The couple looked up to see the hostess. She had the bill in hand, and Jaxson told her they would charge the meal to their room. They finished breakfast and headed out of the restaurant.

"I kinda feel bad about charging a meal to a dead woman," Jaxson whispered as they walked across the lawn toward the mansion.

Holiday pursed her lips. "It's what Daily wanted, dear. And she would be proud to know you've taken up her case."

"I need to start talking to some of the other Crazy Eights," he said.

Holiday looked at her phone. It was just a few minutes before she had to meet her mystery woman in the library.

"Of course. You go do that, and I'll see if this Judith Rainier shows." She gripped his hand tightly as the two made their way up the back steps to the sunroom. "Who do you think you'll talk to first?"

"I guess I'll start with Beau since I already know him. He's a nice guy. Plus, it'll allow me to visit the crime scene."

Holiday took his hands in hers and looked into his eyes. "Be careful, lover. There is a killer among us."

"We both need to be careful."

He kissed her deeply, and Holiday didn't want to let him go. When he pulled away, she went to the library, and a cloud of uncertainty and insecurity settled over her again. All at once, she felt alone and vulnerable.

She'd only taken a few steps down the hall when she heard Leonard calling her name.

"I'm sorry to bother you again," he said. "I have another message for you. It's from Mrs. Pauline Southerleigh. She asked that you call her immediately. She says it's quite urgent, and you would remember her."

Yes, she could never forget the angry voicemail she'd

gotten from Daily's mother after Holiday had returned to Dallas from Charleston. Daily had stopped calling Holiday, but her mother blamed her for breaking up her only child's engagement and for Bobby's death. She'd yelled. She'd cursed. And she'd accused Holiday of sabotaging Daily's life. What would she say now that her only daughter was dead?

"Thank you, Leonard."

Holiday entered the library and stopped short. A woman sat in one of the green-and-taupe checkered high-back chairs next to an open window. A small table was before her, a deck of playing cards spread out in a game of solitaire.

A beige walking cane lay across the woman's wide lap. An unadorned brown purse sat at her feet. She tipped her wine-colored bow cloche and smiled.

"Good morning, Holiday Trousseau," she said in a light, crisp voice. "Do you remember me? I am Judith Rainier."

8
———

How did I get here? Yesterday, I was at a writing conference. Today, I'm interviewing murder suspects.

I plan murders. I don't solve them.

Jaxson paused before Beau's Grand Mansion Suite door. Five suspects. Five interviews. Six if he counted Holiday. Did he count Holiday? He didn't want to believe she could kill Bobby. She'd admitted she'd been in the room the night he died. She'd admitted to over-serving him wine with Midazolam. She said she'd also been knocked out, but since the police dropped her as a suspect, no blood test was ever done. The wine bottle and the glasses that might have incriminated her disappeared, along with the syringe that had injected the tramadol and sertraline. And it had been twenty years since she'd last spoken with the one person investigating Bobby's murder. And then that one person died soon after he and Holiday had arrived at the mansion. Jaxson frowned. Holiday sounded an awful lot like a suspect.

They'd only been married six months. Who really was Holiday Trousseau Bridgewater?

Jaxson knocked, the door swung open, and Beau's broad smile and large silver spectacles met him.

"Sorry that it took me so long." Beau ushered him in. He pointed to the orthopedic boot on his leg. "The doctor told me to have it checked in a couple of weeks, and maybe I'll be free again."

He and Jaxson settled into oversized taupe-colored chairs, a small antique wooden table between them. The bed was made of matching antique cherry wood, with a headboard, footboard, and two nightstands. Beau had opened about a dozen brown shutters that covered the tall windows.

Jaxson searched for a way to begin. Should he ask everyone the same questions and compare the answers? What about a pad and a pencil? He could use his phone for notes. Or no notes? Better to look lost than pretentious.

Beau cut into his thoughts. "How goes the investigation, my friend?"

Jaxson clapped his hands together. "You're the first one I've spoken to. Well, besides my wife, of course."

"Sweet Holiday. Not much of a suspect, that one," Beau said. "I doubt you'll find even the slightest slander in that woman." He looked at Jaxson over the rim of his glasses. "I suppose she told you all the grisly details. It's hard to believe it's been twenty years. And right here in this suite, no less."

Jaxson tried to imagine Holiday in the room. Maybe she and Bobby had sat just like this—Holiday in Jaxson's chair and Bobby in Beau's. Talking and drinking, and Holiday pouring glass after glass until they both passed out. Someone had wanted them drugged.

"How close were you and Bobby?" Jaxson asked.

Beau waved him off. "Barely knew him. We had to

change the name when he joined. The Six Shooters became the Lucky Sevens. And then we became the Crazy Eights."

"Wait, I'm lost," Jaxson said. "You called yourself the Lucky Shooters?"

Beau chuckled. "First, it was just Holiday, Daily, Dave, and me, and we didn't call ourselves anything. We just hung out. Then Dave started dating Payton. That made five. Payton was friends with Tú. That made six. That's when we gave ourselves a name. The Six Shooters."

"Clever."

"Then Bobby came along, and we became the Lucky Sevens. Then came Michael, and we became the Crazy Eights. Can't remember who invited him."

"Was anyone ever declined admission to the group?" Jaxson asked. "Why even have a group like this? What made it, you know, worthwhile?"

"We all had other friends, of course, but none of them said anything about being a part of the group. Most probably thought we were quirky. We were just friends who wanted to get together, drink, and hang out."

Only Holiday had admitted to being at the mansion the night Bobby was killed, and she'd said Tú had come after she called her. But one of the others must have also been in the Grand Mansion Suite if the killer was one of the Crazy Eights.

"Were you here, at the mansion, the night Bobby was killed?"

Beau smiled, but his eyes blinked like a bright light had been thrown behind them. He shook a finger at Jaxson and laughed.

"Not bad, detective. I'm sure you'll find out sooner or later, and there's no reason to hide it. You probably already knew, so yes, I was here."

"You were in Room 10 last time? Same room as yesterday?"

Jaxson looked at the table between them. Was that table here twenty years ago? He looked at the bed in the next room just beyond the oversized pocket doors. Was it the same one where Bobby was found dead?

Probably not. Hotels have to get rid of the bed when something like that happens, don't they?

Beau clicked his tongue and shook his finger at Jaxson again. "Well done, and yes again." He gave Jaxson a sideways glare. "Did Holiday also find it odd to be put up in her same room as last time? Almost as if Daily were trying to make a point."

Beau had known Holiday was at the mansion the night Bobby died, but she hadn't known about Beau. He'd kept it a secret. And how could Daily have known which room everyone was in? One of them must've told her.

"What point would that be? You think Daily was trying to say something?"

Beau frowned. "Oh, I don't know. It just felt like she was rubbing it in our faces. Kinda like the girl who wasn't invited to the party but wanted to show everyone she knew all about it."

"Why were you here that weekend?" Jaxson asked. "I thought it was just a weekend between Holiday and Bobby."

"It was what you might call a business trip." Beau looked at his phone. "Bobby said he had a new opportunity to make serious money in Charleston and wanted to talk about it with me, and I might as well tell you since you're gonna find out anyway, Dave and Michael, too. So, the three of us came out here to meet him, not knowing that he'd brought Holiday along."

Things were making more sense. Almost everyone but

Daily had eventually ended up at the mansion the night Bobby had been killed. What about Payton? Had she come too?

"What was this business opportunity?"

"Never did find out. He was killed before we got the chance to talk to him."

At the very least, Bobby hadn't told Holiday he'd also invited the other three guys when he'd invited her to go to Charleston for the weekend. Had he intended to bring Daily with him? Maybe she'd known of this business opportunity.

"How'd you find out that Bobby was dead?" Jaxson asked.

"The mansion was buzzing when we woke up that morning." Beau rechecked his phone. "Eventually, we learned about Bobby, and well, that was that. We headed back to Dallas."

"Did you see Holiday that weekend?"

"Nope. But we weren't here that long. We checked out early."

"How did you know she was even here if you never saw her?"

Beau's eyes met Jaxson's. "I guess Bobby must've told us. But that wouldn't make sense because we never got to talk to Bobby. Holiday must've told us later that she'd been there, too."

Jaxson shook his head. "Can't be."

Beau squinted and cocked his head.

"Holiday never knew any of you were here that weekend," Jaxson said. "So, if you didn't talk to Bobby and you didn't talk to Holiday, and you two never saw each other, how did you know he'd invited her to be here also?"

Beau drew in a deep breath and laughed it out. "Funny thing about something happening twenty years ago. You don't remember everything." He threw up his hands as if to surrender. "It was such a long time ago. Hard to remember how it all went down, you know?"

Jaxson had just found the first hole in Beau's story, and Beau knew it. But Beau didn't have to know Jaxson knew it, too. Better to play it lost for the time being if it kept everyone talking.

Jaxson nodded. "Believe me, I can't remember half what I did yesterday. I'm discovering that's what wives are for. They have the most amazing memories."

They laughed. Jaxson stood as if to go, and Beau pulled himself up with one of his crutches.

"Let me ask you," Jaxson said, "why do you think someone would want to kill Daily?"

"I think it's clear. One of us killed Bobby, Daily found out, and that same person killed her to keep the secret from getting out."

"I suppose it could've happened like that. I mean, that's what the consensus from this morning was. Still..."

"Do you think it's possible some intruder came in and killed Bobby?" Beau asked. "And maybe Daily just fell, like I did, only she wasn't as fortunate as I was."

Jaxson headed for the door. "It's just that for such a close-knit group as the Crazy Eights, it seems odd that Bobby would invite Holiday and the three guys from the group and not tell you about each other. Makes me wonder. Was that weekend about business or pleasure for Bobby Boudreaux?"

"You know what they say..." Beau extended his hand to Jaxson, and they shook by the open door. "Never mix business with pleasure. Maybe that was Bobby's way of keeping the two separate."

Jaxson gave him a slight chuckle. "Could be. But then,

which was which? Was Holiday his pleasure or his business?"

Beau opened his mouth to say something, but nothing came out, and Jaxson turned and headed into the lobby.

————

The library wasn't really a library. The walls weren't lined with books, and there was no free-standing globe on a polished mahogany stand in the middle of the room. Instead, a small credenza sat at one end of the rectangular room with a laptop, a green librarian's lamp, and a stack of puzzles and games. It was not exactly the sort of thing Holiday imagined when reading one of Agatha Christie's mysteries.

Still, a dead body could fit in the room, that is, if the body were turned longways. If Jaxson wished to use the Wentworth for one of their mysteries, he'd have to use some other room to find a body.

Judith's outfit was as unassuming as her nature: loose-fitting light blue pants, black athletic shoes with thick rubber soles, and a long-sleeved white knit shirt with black polka dots. A gold cross chain hung around her neck. Her brown eyes lit up when Holiday entered the room.

"It's a shame the owner doesn't serve morning wine and hors d'oeuvres," Judith Rainier mused. "I've mentioned this to them several times, but I'm afraid my suggestions have gone unappreciated."

Judith scooped up the playing cards and handed the box to Holiday, who placed it on the library's shelves, along with the other games.

"I used to be quite the card shark back in my day," said Judith.

Holiday found it curious that the woman, whom she had only passed outside the elevator, would want to talk. Perhaps Mrs. Rainier had recognized Holiday from some of the advertisement work she'd done for her father's business. She didn't think they'd ever met beforehand. Still, there was something familiar about Mrs. Rainier, and Holiday wanted to settle her mind about it. She'd listen to what Judith had to say and then get back to helping Jaxson find Daily's killer.

"Imagine my surprise when I saw you yesterday." Judith leaned her cane against the chair. "At first, I couldn't place you. It took me all night. It wasn't until I'd heard about the young woman dying that it came to me who you were. I still have a good memory. It just takes a little longer to fire it up sometimes."

Holiday struggled to place the woman, and she jogged back through her most recent memories for a place or an event that might explain where the two had previously met. "I'm afraid I don't remember you, Mrs. Rainier."

"Of course you don't, my dear, and please call me Judith. It was such a long time ago. You were so young with a head full of love, but just as beautiful then as you are now. And you probably thought I was already just another old woman. Well, I wasn't as old then as I am now. I was sixty-four the first time we met." Judith looked outside the window. "Arthur and I loved coming here."

"Arthur. He was your husband?"

Judith smiled. "He passed three years ago this January. I didn't think I could return here after that, but I did. I forced myself, you see. Every late October, I stay in Room 9, just as Arthur and I did for twenty-two years."

Holiday looked at the woman's sweet face, the deep wrinkles etched softly into her skin. "Would you be so kind as to remind me where we met?"

Judith nodded. "In the parlor, the day after you checked in. You were here with the young man who later died. My Arthur was with us, and you said your young fellow had gone back upstairs to check on something. He was gone for a good half hour, and you began to worry about him. Just then, he returned, and the two of you headed out for a day's adventure."

Memories returned. The parlor. The conversation. Waiting on Bobby. Talking to the older couple who reminded her of her grandparents, the way they had held hands and kissed. Judith was correct. Bobby had been gone a long time after he'd said it would take just a moment.

"I remember something you told me," Holiday said. "You said that finding the love of your life is like pairing the right wine with your meal."

Judith smiled. "You must take a lot of sips before you know what to fill your glass with. I told you not to rush. Did you rush?"

Holiday felt a slight flutter in her stomach. "I waited. I sipped from a lot of glasses until I found the most amazing man. His name is Jaxson."

"Good for you, sweet girl." Judith let out a slow breath. "I was fifty-six when Arthur and I married. People said I waited too long, but Arthur was the love of my life. He knew me. And when we found Wentworth, we started coming every year in October to celebrate our anniversary. We spent twenty-two anniversaries here." She looked wistfully outside the window. "And we're still celebrating them."

"I love that story. And I want you to meet Jaxson. You're the reason I found him—because I waited."

Judith squeezed her hand. "You are no longer just Holiday Trousseau now."

"Holiday Trousseau Bridgewater." Another flutter

passed through her. How did Jaxson do that to her, even when he wasn't around?

"Bridgewater." Judith closed her eyes and smiled as she tried out the name. "Strong and sturdy. The name suits you perfectly. What a lucky man he is to have found you. I want to meet him, dear girl. Arthur would've wanted to meet him, too. But there's another reason I wanted to see you today. It's about the death of that young man you came here with twenty years ago."

Holiday uncrossed her legs and leaned forward. "Bobby?"

Judith lowered her voice and nodded. "You weren't the only woman he was with that night."

Holiday stared at Judith, not daring to breathe. Did Daily come with Bobby that night as well? "Another woman?"

Judith looked around and whispered. "His wife."

J axson was eager to find another member of the Crazy Eights and corroborate the discoveries he'd already made. Starting with Beau had been a wise choice. It'd given him a chance to warm up his interview skills on the most benign member, and he'd also gained some solid intel about the night Bobby died. Still, it had bothered Jaxson that he hadn't gone with Holiday to meet her mystery guest. Before seeking out his next victim, he decided he'd pop his head into the library to check on Holiday first. Leonard stopped him before the elevator.

"Mr. Bridgewater. I just came from the fourth floor, where I was taking stock of the cupola, when I noticed the door to your room was open. I wouldn't normally, but I took the liberty to step into your room due to last night's circumstances. It would appear as though your belongings have been gone through."

"Gone through?" Jaxson widened his eyes.

"Ransacked is the word, I believe. Burgled, perhaps." He cleared his throat. "Your room is a mess."

A tinge of embarrassment swept over Jaxson. He and Holiday were attracting drama at the dignified Wentworth. It hadn't occurred to him that someone might retaliate for his investigation. And in the middle of the morning, just a few floors up from where Holiday was meeting with Judith Rainier. Was someone already trying to drive him and Holiday off the case?

He didn't wait for the elevator. He took the grand staircase two steps at a time and found their room just as Leonard had described.

Somebody had given it a good going over. Their suitcases were overturned, their clothes spread across the floor. The bed had been stripped, the comforter, sheets, and pillows piled near the fireplace. His computer bag had been dumped, but his laptop sat neatly on the antique desk. Holiday's jewelry had been dumped on the nightstand.

In the bathroom, someone had emptied their toiletries in the shower.

And there was a message written in shaving cream on the small mirror above the sink.

Go home!

Jaxson sat on the edge of the garden tub and studied the mess strewn about their room. Was it just a warning, or was someone looking for something?

Either way, someone was getting nervous.

Beau had no doubt texted the other four to relay how his interrogation had gone. What to say, what not to say.

The group had been a bit cagey when they'd asked him to investigate Daily's death, as though they'd wanted him to search for answers that they hoped he'd never find.

What about Holiday? If she wanted to abandon the investigation, he could fly her back, get her out of harm's way. But it would be without him. He had more interviews to conduct.

He picked up the phone and dialed Leonard. "Would you send your housekeeper up when you have a chance? We need some new linens and fresh towels."

Leonard said he would straightaway.

"One more thing," Jaxson said, "ask her not to clean the bathroom mirror. Someone's left me a message, and I want to keep it for a while."

Jaxson sat on the edge of the garden tub again and studied the message on the mirror.

There was something odd about it—not with the message itself but with the letters. They looked familiar, particularly the exclamation point, which was very stylized. The writer had used a circle instead of a solid dot.

He knew that writing style—circles on top of i's and in the place of ellipses and punctuation marks.

A vertical line extending longer than the last letter with a circle beneath it.

"Holiday makes her exclamation points like this," he said aloud.

He took a picture of the message with his phone.

9

___

"What do you mean, his wife?" Holiday asked Judith. Had Bobby and Daily gotten married after all, without telling anyone? Holiday thought back to all the attempts Daily had made to reach her that day. Daily had been trying to tell her that Bobby was her husband.

Judith reached for her cane and held it while she spoke. "As I recall, you two were in the parlor. I was in the sunroom and overheard you and Mr. Boudreaux speaking with Mr. McAnelly, the innkeeper at the time, about his getting another room. I remember thinking, 'Good girl. She's not rushing it.'"

Why wouldn't Daily have told her? Had she regretted her decision to marry so soon? Maybe she was embarrassed. But then again, Daily never made snap decisions. She never got embarrassed. And she never regretted anything.

"Where did you see this woman who said she was his wife?"

"Several hours later, I was still in the sunroom reading when this beautiful young woman came in looking for Mr. Boudreaux. I asked if she was his friend, and when she said 'wife,' I almost fell over. She had the prettiest smile. She was dressed nicely and had a lovely black purse over her shoulder. And she was very soft-spoken. I told her he was just around the corner in the Grand Mansion Suite. She thanked me and left."

The words stuck in Holiday's throat. "That's impossible. We all would've known about her. What did she look like?"

"She had black hair and was very slender, very much like you, but with darker skin, as I recall." Judith let out a little sigh. "I'm quite good with faces, you know. My Arthur always said I was."

Dark hair. That wasn't Daily. Bobby had married someone else. Had Daily known?

"There's one more thing," Judith said, "and it has to do with the three gentlemen who came to see Mr. Boudreaux."

Were there more people looking for Bobby at the mansion that day? How could she not have known this? "What did these three men say?"

"They stayed in Room 10 next to us. Arthur said he knew they were up to no good. Why would three young men stay at Wentworth all crowded up in one bedroom, he asked me. Where did one of them even sleep? In the bathtub? I told Arthur it was none of our business, but we noticed them just the same."

"Did you get their names?" Holiday asked. "Did they say anything about hurting Bobby?"

"They were young men like Mr. Boudreaux. Arthur also went upstairs while you and I talked that day, as you waited for Mr. Boudreaux. When you and Mr. Boudreaux left for your outing, I went upstairs. Arthur was waiting for me at the door, and I could tell he was disturbed. He said Mr. Boudreaux had just been in the room with the three men, and there had been a great deal of shouting and yelling.

Arthur eventually went to the door and asked if everything was okay. Mr. Boudreaux said they were disagreeing, and they'd hold it down. After that, we didn't hear a peep. When we woke up in the morning, the housekeeper was cleaning the room, and they were gone."

Holiday sat back in her chair and crossed her arms. Bobby had suddenly needed to go upstairs to get his wallet, and he'd been gone a long time. Judith's story made sense. Bobby had used his wallet as an excuse to talk with the three men in Room 10, and he hadn't wanted Holiday to know.

"You said the men were young. What did these men look like?" Holiday asked.

"That's the thing," said Judith. She used her cane to lean closer to Holiday and whispered. "They're here again."

Holiday's mouth flew open. "They are? Here at the inn? Do they work here?"

"I don't think so. You seem to know them. I saw all of you together at dinner last night. They were the same men Mr. Boudreaux argued with the day he was killed."

Michael, Dave, and Beau had also been at the mansion that day. They were there when Bobby died. They were there when Daily died, too.

And they had argued with Bobby. Is this what Daily had discovered? Was she killed to keep the rest from finding out that one of them, two of them, all of them, had killed Bobby?

"I had to meet with you," Judith said. "When you jumped up from the table last night and ran out, the man beside you, who I assume is your husband, and the two other women were shocked. But the three men didn't flinch. They looked at each other as if they had a secret between them."

Judith pulled up her cane and slowly rose to her feet. Holiday stood, too. She saw Jaxson sitting down with Payton in the garden behind the house.

"You be careful, Mrs. Holiday Trousseau Bridgewater," Judith said. "I believed my Arthur then, and I believe him now. Those three men are up to no good."

J axson found Payton on a black wrought iron bench, scrolling through her phone in the shade of a large southern magnolia. Holiday had said Dave and Payton had gotten married before they'd graduated. He wondered if Payton had known her husband was at the mansion with Bobby, Beau, and Michael, and if she was aware of the business opportunity Bobby was planning. He suspected she knew something and was present that night, just like the rest. They'd all jumped when Daily made the invitation, Payton included.

"Mind if I join you?" he asked.

Her eyes widened, and she jammed her phone in her coat pocket. "You want to ask me some questions? I'm afraid I can't help you all that much. I wasn't here back when Bobby died."

"He didn't just die. He was killed. And you were here, weren't you?" Jaxson leaned in. "The night Bobby was murdered."

Payton looked at the broad, white steps leading up to the house's back door. "Should I get a lawyer?" she asked, her voice breaking.

Jaxson tried to stifle a strangled laugh. "Sorry. I'm not arresting you. I'm just asking some questions about that night." He leaned back and crossed his legs. "If it helps,

Beau told me that he, Michael, and Dave were here. Something about a business deal Bobby was working on."

"He did? He told you?" Payton's eyes darted again to the back entrance of the inn. "So, yeah, that's all I knew, too. I think they all got here a day before me. Dave said the guys would talk business, and the rest of the weekend would be like a second honeymoon for us. It was our first time in Charleston and our only time until now."

"You didn't sense anything out of the ordinary about the weekend? Just your new husband meeting in a city you'd never been to with three college friends about a business venture? What did you think about Bobby?"

Holiday emerged from the sunroom and sat down on the back steps. She smiled at him and interlocked her fingers like praying hands, dropping her chin on them. He resisted the urge to smile back when he saw Payton glance at Holiday. Payton shifted on the bench, crossing her legs, her back turned slightly more toward the house.

"You didn't much like him?" Jaxson ventured. "It's okay if you didn't."

She shrugged. Her eyes focused on the small palmetto tree just a few feet away.

Jaxson lowered his voice. "Or maybe you did."

Payton leaned toward Jaxson. "Bobby had photos of me. Inappropriate photos. The kind of photos you don't want your parents, friends, or children to see."

"Or your new husband?"

She closed her eyes and nodded without looking up. "Bobby said he needed *collateral* for this new business opportunity. He said I was his collateral. He said if I didn't want those photos released, the best thing I could do was stay out of his business and keep Dave in it."

A gentle breeze blew across the yard, bending the deep

red Noisette roses that climbed up the tall, white trellis in the garden bed near the mansion's side steps where Holiday sat. Her hair blew across her face, and she brushed it behind her ear with a finger.

"You have to understand," said Payton, "I was a first-grade teacher, just starting out, and Bobby said if I destroyed his career, he would destroy mine."

"Did he mention what this business opportunity was?"

The back door of the sunroom flew open. Dave stormed out. "Hey! No! Don't talk to her without me!"

Dave raced down the steps and nearly tripped over Holiday. He was panting hard. "He has no business getting into our affairs, especially things that happened twenty years ago that don't pertain to Daily."

Jaxson removed his hands from his pocket. "You guys asked me to investigate."

"If you need to talk to us, you do it with both of us together. Got it?" Dave turned to his wife. "What did you tell him?"

Payton was shaking. "I...Just about—"

"Dave," Jaxson said, "how about we all just sit down and talk about things together?"

"No, we're not gonna sit down and talk about things. The group might've wanted you to investigate, but I voted against it. Don't talk to my wife again." He turned toward the house, pulling Payton with him.

Holiday came over to Jaxson. "I think you hit a nerve."

"I hit something for sure." He leaned in and kissed her. "I have a lot to tell you. How about we walk downtown to Peninsula Grill for lunch and catch up there?"

She grabbed his hand. "I have a lot to tell you, too. It's a date. Let me grab my purse."

"About that..." He told her about the mess in their room,

the message on the mirror, and the stylized exclamation point.

She crossed her arms. "I was afraid of this. I know who wrote that message. I knew it could be awkward, but I didn't think she'd go this far... She thinks I did it."

Jaxson squeezed her hand. "Who are we talking about?"

"Tú. She and I are the only Crazy Eights who punctuate with circles. Even that night when she came to rescue me, I could tell she thought I had killed Bobby. Now that we're all back, she's probably looking for evidence."

"Do you think she could've killed Daily?"

"I can't see it. But I can't see her destroying our room either. None of this makes sense."

Holiday pointed across the back lawn. Tú was sitting under an umbrella outside the spa in a white robe. "Here's your chance. Why don't you ask her?"

"I think I will."

Holiday lifted her phone. "I think I will make a call."

H oliday steeled herself for new accusations. She would let Daily's mother talk. She would be polite. And then, she would get back to finding Bobby and Daily's killer.

Mrs. Southerleigh answered on the third ring.

"Oh, Holiday, please say it isn't true."

Holiday swallowed hard. She fought the sudden urge to cry. "I'm sorry, Mrs. Southerleigh. It's..."

Her voice broke. She could hear Mrs. Southerleigh sobbing, her grief pouring through soft moans.

Holiday cried with her. "I...know...it's so..." The words blocked her throat, choking her.

It was the first time Holiday had allowed herself to grieve since waking. All morning, she'd been emboldened by a sense of purpose to find Bobby and Daily's killer. But feelings of deep sadness now bubbled to the surface. She would never see Daily again. Her heart hurt. Her body shook. And the tears streamed unrelentingly over her cheeks.

Finally, Mrs. Southerleigh managed to get out a complete sentence. "The police say she fell coming down a spiral staircase. Is that correct?"

"That's what they're saying."

The woman was crying again, and Holiday waited, silent tears pouring over her cheeks.

"It was at the same inn where Bobby died?" her mother managed between sobs.

"Yes."

"And the same weekend?"

Her mother remembered.

"Yes."

"Holiday?"

"Yes, Mrs. Southerleigh?"

"Do you think Daily was murdered because of Bobby?"

Holiday was unsure what to say, afraid to say anything that might bring further pain to the grieving mother.

"You do," Mrs. Southerleigh said. "The police think it was just an unfortunate accident, but you think someone murdered her because she knew who killed Bobby."

Holiday stole a glance behind her. Jaxson was gone, and so was Tú. "My husband, Jaxson, is trying to figure out what happened, Mrs. Southerleigh."

"I saw you got married. Daily was so happy for you when we heard."

"She was?" Holiday's heart began to race, and she bit her

lip to keep the tears from falling from her eyes. It didn't help.

"She never stopped loving you, Holiday."

Holiday flashed back to the secret message on the mirror. "I know," she said, just above a whisper. "Mrs. Southerleigh, did Daily ever mention why Bobby broke up with her?"

"Bobby didn't break up with her. She broke up with him."

Her words stopped Holiday. If this were true, it would mean Daily, and not Holiday, was supposed to be at the mansion that weekend. "Are you sure?"

"I'm positive. She told me all about it."

Bobby had lied, not just about who had broken up with whom, but also about his feelings for Holiday.

He hadn't called off his engagement to Daily and taken Holiday to Charleston because he loved her. He'd brought her because Daily wouldn't come. Holiday had been his second choice—runner-up.

"Did she tell you why?" Holiday asked.

"As I understand, it had to do with drugs, honey. She found out he was using, and Daily wanted no part of it. She confronted him, and he denied it, of course. But you know Daily. Once she got her teeth in a bone, she wouldn't let it go. He finally admitted it. He'd wanted her to go to Charleston with him for a romantic weekend, but she said she wasn't going and broke off their engagement. That was the last time they spoke."

"Mrs. Southerleigh, I know this is a painful time. Did Daily ever mention to you anything about Bobby's murder? Anything she might've discovered?"

"No, she kept that part of her life closed off. I knew she would investigate it occasionally. I didn't like the idea that she'd decided to open a gallery in the same city where her former fiancé had died. However, she was a highly successful artist. The city was good to her. And we never talked about the past much, only about her plans. Did you know she was going to open a second gallery?"

That's right. Daily had a gallery where she might've kept notes on her investigation.

"No, I did not. Would you mind texting me the address?"

"I'll do it as soon as we hang up. I'm sorry, but I don't have the keys. Maybe someone at the gallery can help you. Thank you, Holiday, for calling me. And thank you for looking into her death. The police don't believe it, but my heart tells me that her death has something to do with Bobby's murder."

"Mine, too. Goodbye, Mrs. Southerleigh, and thank you."

Holiday had been afraid Pauline Southerleigh would blame her for Daily's murder. Instead, she had shed new light on Bobby's.

One of the Crazy Eights had come back, not to catch a killer, but to kill again.

10

Two mimosas had worked miracles on Tú's disposition. She was snuggled up in a plush white robe, black rubber sandals on her feet. Her cat eye sunglasses covered her eyes, but her black mask was pulled down to her chin, and she smiled when she saw Jaxson. She kicked one of the chairs out from the table for him and lifted her drink.

"I only wish I could thank our dearly departed fellow Eight for all my self-love this morning." She took another sip. "That was kind of dark, wasn't it?"

Jaxson stood before the table. "I'm not one to judge others' motives."

She scoffed. "*Au contraire,* my good man. Isn't that the very thing you were elected to do this morning? Judge us all as you root out the evil among us? For the record, I was in favor of bringing you on board."

He tipped his head toward her. "Thank you for that vote of confidence."

"It wasn't confidence," she said. "I actually don't think you'll find anything of consequence. You're just a teacher, for God's sake, not the second coming of Hercule Poirot. My vote was merely a matter of curiosity."

Jaxson laughed. "You sound like the parents back in my classroom days, and as I said to them, I promise not to hold your inability to become a teacher against you." He sat across from her. "You're merely curious as to who killed two of your own in the same mansion exactly twenty years apart?"

She waved an indifferent hand at his suggestion. "I'm with the police on this one. Bobby's death was a random murder, and Daily's was an unfortunate accident. But I'm most curious what our little Holiday has found in you." She cut her eyes over her sunglasses. "Who are you really, Mr. Jaxson Bridgewater? Where did you come from all of a sudden?"

Jaxson cast a wary eye on the woman. "I'm not sure I know what you mean."

"The rest of us marry and divorce and make a glorious mess of our lives, stumbling around with self-inflicted wounds from one horrendous disaster to the next. But not our Holiday. Nope! Nobody was ever good enough for Miss Holiday Trousseau. She's a careful one, that girl. And then suddenly this...teacher—"

"...school administrator."

She waved him off again. "And suddenly, our little Holiday has not only fallen in love but gotten herself married." She leaned closer and lowered her voice. "And the word on the street is that Daddy wasn't too thrilled about her choice either. You pulled off what no other man or woman has been able to do. Trust me when I say there's been no lack of suitors in Miss Holiday Trousseau's life. So, I ask again, Mr. Jaxson Bridgewater. Who are you?"

It was a legitimate question. Who was he to be getting

involved in the drama of six adults he'd barely met twelve hours earlier? They knew even less about him, but maybe that was the point. Had they all felt the same, curious about him and Holiday, indifferent to Bobby and Daily? Perhaps they already knew their killer, and their charge was just a frivolous MacGuffin meant to elicit the true nature of his and Holiday's relationship. Or possibly Holiday was right. Perhaps they suspected her and figured the closest one to her might be the best one to uncover the evidence against her. They wanted him to do their dirty work.

"How'd I get to be so lucky with Holiday?" Jaxson shrugged. "I ask myself that all the time, Miss Dinh."

She sat back in her chair, crossed her arms, and pulled at the mask under her chin. "You must call me Tú. But seriously, Jax, you don't fool me. Men of your stature don't just fall into marriage with one of the wealthiest heiresses in the country."

"Tú, I'm just a simple man who loves a good mystery and happened to be in the right place at the right time."

"You're also deceptively intuitive. Before others realize it, you've wormed your way into their souls and confidences. I like that about you, Jax. But remember this. A man will only succeed to the degree that the most powerful woman in his life will allow."

"Do you have a man who makes you that woman, Tú?"

She laughed. "There have been several who wanted me to believe I was that woman and now find themselves in the wake of my success. But to your question, there is one, and only time will tell if he succeeds where others have failed. But a discussion concerning my romantic attachments isn't what you want."

"I was wondering if I might ask you a question or two about Bobby's murder."

She extended her arms toward him with flair. "You picked a most fortunate time. I'm already too drunk to care what you think about me and am liable to say whatever pops into my head. I'm quite unguarded, Jax, in so many ways that would alarm your little wifey."

Jaxson looked back at Holiday. She was on the phone, but she was watching him and Tú.

Tú went on. "I don't mind answering your questions, but you'll have to do it during my ninety-minute massage." She looked at her watch. "I'm due now. Come on."

She handed one of her mimosas to Jaxson, and he followed her through the spa's front door and down the long, dark brick hall that once had been part of the mansion's stables. The attendant ushered them to a young therapist waiting outside the massage room.

The therapist studied her chart. "I'm sorry, Miss Dinh, but I don't have your husband down for a couple's massage."

Tú sipped her drink and brushed past the therapist. "Oh, it's all good, honey. He's not getting a massage. And he's not my husband."

Tú waved Jaxson in, took the mimosa from his hand, and set it on the counter.

"You two can stay. There's nothing I'm ashamed of." Tú dropped the robe to the floor and motioned toward the massage table. "Face up or down, missy?"

The therapist stood frozen in the doorway, her mouth open.

Jaxson raised an eyebrow. "Do you want her face up or face down to begin?"

"Face down," the therapist said in a tiny voice.

Jaxson shrugged at Tú. "She says face down." He tried not to stare at her breasts, but they were quite large, and she'd kept her body in excellent shape.

Tú winked and got on the table. "In case you were wondering, they are as natural as I am."

The therapist draped a sheet over Tú's body and set to work.

"You said you had some questions for me?" She angled her head toward the therapist. "Everything you're hearing is off the record. Understood? I'm happy to settle in court if one word of this conversation goes viral. Think of yourself as a counselor, not a mere massage therapist. Non-disclosure and all. Got it?"

The therapist's hands stopped, and she nodded at Tú, her eyes wide.

Tú laughed. "I like talking to you, Jax. May I call you Jax?"

"A lot of people do."

"Good. I can see why Holiday married you, besides your good looks. You've got a charming way of disarming the guarded. Of course, it doesn't hurt that I've already had some good mimosas. Now, what was it you wanted to know?"

Jaxson looked around the small, dark room and found a chair in the corner. "Where were you the night Bobby died?"

"Oh, for God's sake, ask me something you don't already know. I'm sure your wife told you I was at my grandmother's when Holiday called and told me what happened, and I came by."

"That was nice of you to come to her aid when she called. She said you were the first she thought of."

Tú made a slight groan as the therapist worked on the back of one of her legs. "Oh, yes, right there. My hamstring gets so tight from running." She paused. "That was nice of Holiday, although I think it was more of a practical decision than anything else."

"She said you two went back into the room after you arrived. Why was that?"

"Again, I refer you back to your wife."

Jaxson smiled. "You're refreshingly brisk. I'm surprised you didn't go into law after all."

"I tried it and found it insufferably boring. I can't tolerate BS. I call it like I see it."

"Did it not bother you to see a dead body when you and Holiday entered the room that night?"

"I didn't look at him. We were there to wipe it down, see if she'd lost anything, and get out. We weren't there for more than three or four minutes. Maybe less."

"How did you two get in?"

"We came in through the front door. Believe it or not, it was unlocked."

"And you left the same way? Through the front door?"

She nodded. "We left through the front and took the elevator back to the fourth floor. It was a spooky ride up, too. Suddenly, it stopped, and the lights went out. I thought we'd been discovered, but then it went on. I spent the night with her in that room. The whole affair quite shook her. I felt for the girl, I really did."

"She told me you were her alibi."

Tú nodded. "I told her she had nothing to worry about if nobody had seen her go in and out of the room. Back then, there weren't cameras everywhere, and we were each other's witnesses."

Jaxson didn't like the idea that his new wife had never admitted to the police that she'd once left the scene of a murder. But had she stayed and called the police, wouldn't she have automatically become the prime suspect? If it hadn't been for Tú's quick thinking, Holiday's prints would have been all over the room. The innkeeper would've testified that Holiday had been with the victim earlier in the day, and they must've had a lovers' spat since they were now in separate rooms. And Holiday was the one who poured the drugged wine for Bobby. Holiday would've satisfied it all—means, motive, and opportunity.

But where was the murder weapon? She and Tú hadn't located the syringe. Either someone had gone into the room between the two times Holiday had been there, or, perhaps even more probable, Tú and Holiday hadn't found it. What if the killer had quickly discarded the syringe in the room? Behind a dresser? Into the wall where the pocket doors slide? In the fireplace? Suddenly, Jaxson had an urge to revisit the Grand Mansion Suite.

"Did you know that Beau, Michael, and Dave were here that night also?" he asked.

"Not until much later. Michael told me about him and the others. He's a good man, a sweet soul. And he's a mean cook. He makes the best coq au vin."

"I'll have to get the recipe. Did you know Holiday would be here that night?"

"Bobby told me he'd broken up with Daily, and he and Holiday were going to have a romantic weekend here." She grimaced as the therapist worked on her other leg.

"Do you know why the others were here?" Jaxson asked.

"Michael said it had to do with a business opportunity, but they realized Bobby's idea had gone belly up once they'd arrived. Then, when Bobby died, they left."

Jaxson found the front door to the Grand Mansion Suite bothersome. It was probably why the police had called the murder a random killing. The killer could've just slipped in and out of the front door without anyone in the rest of the inn being aware. But would Bobby have left it unlocked? Was he expecting a guest to enter that way?

"Would you like to see the last photo of The Crazy Eights?" Tú asked through the hole in the headrest. "Get my phone out of my robe. There's no passcode. I added the photo just the other day."

Jaxson retrieved her phone and opened the photos app. The three most recent pictures were nudes of Tú. The fourth was a group photo of the Crazy Eights on the observation deck of Reunion Tower in downtown Dallas with the city skyline in the background. They were dressed identically in white SMU tees and blue jeans, aside from the long silver chains and loop earrings the women wore. Tú wore a gold rope bracelet on her wrist like the one Holiday had discovered in Daily's room. Daily had a sizable silver diamond on her wedding finger. They were younger and thinner, and their smiles were full of fresh optimism.

Tú raised her head. "We looked pretty good back then, didn't we?"

"You all still look good. Do you mind if I send myself this photo?"

"Text away." She turned to the therapist. "Your hands are magical. I can't wait for you to get hold of my arms."

Jaxson felt his phone buzz with the incoming photo. Then it buzzed again. He pulled it out and saw a message from a number he didn't recognize.

Need to talk. Meet me at the bar in Circa 1886. Michael

Michael had been the one at breakfast to say everyone in the group had a secret to hide. So far, Holiday had been the only one who had admitted to hiding anything. Everyone seemed to know Holiday's secret, but nobody could remember their own.

He put Tú's phone back into her robe. "Just one more question, if you don't mind."

"Don't rush off on my account," she said.

"I found a message on our bathroom mirror today. Any idea who might've written it?"

Tú's face was back up, and she waved at the therapist to stop. "What kind of message?"

"'Go home' with an exclamation point behind it."

She laughed. "Let me guess. The exclamation point had a circle at the bottom instead of a dot. Is that right? And your wife said I was the one who made my exclamation points like that. Correct?"

Jaxson nodded.

"She's right. I do. I use those little circles on top of the letter *i* and for periods and exclamation points. It just seems more fun-looking, you know? Holiday does it, too. Now, if you're wondering if I wrote the note, the answer is no. And I doubt Holiday did either. But I agree with the note. You two need to go back to Dallas."

"You want me to stop poking around in the past?" Jaxson asked. "What about Bobby? Daily?"

There was a long pause until, at last, Tú said, "You know, I think I will enjoy the rest of my massage in peace." She lowered her head into the pillow rest again. "I think you've seen enough of me today."

Jaxson edged his way around the front of the massage table. Tú grabbed his legs, holding him tight around his thighs.

She raised her head. "Funny thing about secrets, Jaxson Bridgewater. They're all connected. You can't just dig up one. We all have them, you know. You, me, your wife. And the thing you gotta ask yourself is this: *Am I willing to dig up everyone else's darkest secret even if it means exposing the deep-*

est, most vile secret of the woman I love? Trust me when I say this. Holiday Trousseau hasn't told you everything. If she had, you wouldn't be here, talking to me. You'd pack it up and do exactly what that message said. Some secrets are better left buried."

Jaxson felt his stomach turn. They'd all been guilty of something that night, and only Holiday had been willing to share it. But what if she'd only told him enough to get him on her side? What if getting Bobby drunk wasn't the worst crime she'd committed in the Grand Mansion Suite twenty years ago?

Tú let go of Jaxson, and he headed for the door.

Holiday was sitting at the black iron table on the garden patio when she saw Jaxson striding toward her across the backyard. White polo. Navy blue twill pants. His brown leather jacket and fedora. He dressed so much better since she'd started shopping for him.

Telling him everything about the night Bobby was killed had been liberating. He hadn't sounded disappointed in her. Still, six months into their marriage, she had discovered her new husband didn't always say what he was thinking. She couldn't believe she'd told Jaxson she'd gotten a man so drunk and defenseless that someone could kill him. It was almost as if the killer had used her to do half the job. But how had someone known she would be in that room? Had she been set up to take the fall for Bobby's murder? If it hadn't been for Tú that night...

"One more person to talk to before lunch." Jaxson took the chair beside her. "But first, tell me about your conversation with this Judith Rainier."

Holiday caught him up on the argument Judith's husband had overhead inside Room 10 and Bobby's mysterious wife. Jaxson's eyes were wide when she told him of her conversation with Daily's mother.

"Wow. I didn't see that one coming," he said. "Sounds like Bobby was on the rebound when he invited you to join him for the weekend." He glanced at his watch. "We need to visit with our next suspect, and this time, you're coming with me."

Her heart began to race. Her first interview of a fellow Eight. It might look like coercion, her being with him during an interview. If they blamed her for Bobby's death, would they now accuse her of manipulating Jaxson to make sure he didn't blame her as well?

She followed Jaxson toward the mansion's restaurant. "Are you sure you shouldn't talk to everyone alone, dear? I am a suspect in this whole business, too."

He squeezed her hand as they walked. "You're not a suspect. You're my Watson."

She kissed him on his scruffy face. "I love being your Watson, Mr. Sherlock Bridgewater."

He smirked at her and stopped at the restaurant's pergola entryway. "Michael's the only one I haven't spoken with. Well, if you don't count Dave."

Holiday rolled her eyes. "I don't recall ever seeing him so angry. And did you see Payton's face? She was frightened. The happy couple? Ha!" She looked at the restaurant. "This place is just beautiful. I can't believe it used to be the stables."

They made their way down the lily turf-lined brick walkway to the doors of Circa 1886.

"We have to go to lunch after this," Holiday said. "I'm starving."

Jaxson raised an eyebrow. "Didn't we just have breakfast?"

She shrugged. "Sleuthing makes me hungry."

"Sleuthing?" He laughed as he held the door for her, and she scrunched her nose at him as she passed through.

They found Michael at the bar inside, a beer between his hands. Nobody else was around.

"Now, this is a restaurant," Michael said without turning.

The bar exuded the same Southern charm as the formal dining room. Moss-green high-back chairs were pulled up neatly to a black marble bar. An assortment of spirits, liqueurs, and glassware lined the white, mirrored back bar that ran the length of the rear wall. A cute bistro table with a dimly lit brass light was placed before a gray Venetian plaster fireplace. And the original pine floor was stained a light burlap.

Jaxson took the seat next to Michael, and Holiday sat beside Jaxson.

"You enjoyed the meal last night?" Jaxson asked.

"I know the chef," Michael said. "There's no one better in the business. No restaurant is better anywhere."

"You speak with some authority on the matter," Jaxson observed.

"I have a place in Houston now. Nothing big. TexMex fine dining."

"I thought so," Holiday said. "Didn't you major in business?"

"Only because I had to choose something. I always knew it would be either law enforcement or culinary arts. I like to eat, so it was a no-brainer. But mostly, I like to make money." He nursed his beer. "I want you to know I am on board with your investigation into Daily's death. I was serious about what I said over breakfast this morning. You weren't here when it happened. That makes you the only one of us who's not a suspect." Michael winked at Holiday.

"I'm glad you brought that up," Jaxson said. "We've learned that Bobby and Holiday weren't alone here at the mansion the night he died. You, Beau, and Dave were here. And Payton eventually."

"You're right," Michael said. "And when Daily set up this weekend, she put some of us back in our same rooms."

"You were in Room 10 twenty years ago," Jaxson said.

Michael nodded. "Beau, Dave, and I didn't have any money, so we split Room 10 three ways. We were only here one night. The next day, we were gone."

"You left after Bobby died," Jaxson said.

Michael held up his index finger. "We left after the police said we could."

"Why did the three of you meet Bobby here?" Holiday asked.

"Bobby said he had a business opportunity that could make us all a lot of money. It turned out to be a dud. Unfortunately for Bobby, the weekend only got worse from there."

"What kind of opportunity?" Jaxson asked. "I'm sure it wasn't selling encyclopedias door-to-door."

Michael gave a long shrug. "Search me. He was dead before he filled us in."

Jaxson narrowed his eyes. "You said it was a dud. How could you know that if he hadn't filled you in? Sorry to be picky, but you asked me to do this."

Michael looked at the fireplace at the end of the bar. "I get it, but you gotta admit, it was long ago, Jaxson. Had you asked me back then, I would've probably remembered."

"And what about the argument you guys had that morning?"

"What argument?"

Holiday spoke up. "Someone overheard an argument in

Room 10 the morning you, Dave, and Beau were there. Was the argument about Bobby?"

"Seriously, I have no idea what you're talking about. If there was an argument, I wasn't there. If it was that morning, I'd gone to the old downtown to look around. Ask the other two guys. They'll tell you if they remember."

Holiday flashed back to the day she first met Michael, back in Dallas. The group had decided to bike the nine-mile path around White Rock Lake one Saturday morning, and just like that, Michael had suddenly made them the Crazy Eights. She couldn't remember who had invited him, but he'd been more mature than the other three guys back then. He was more serious, more intense. And he never seemed to be entirely satisfied with the moment. Twenty years later, he still had that uneasy vibe about him. Would Michael ever find what he was looking for?

"Can you tell me why you all were here, of all weekends, at the same time as Bobby and Holiday?" Jaxson asked.

"It was all Bobby's idea." He turned to Holiday. "We didn't know you were going to be here until..."

Holiday leaned in. "Until what?"

Michael shook his head. "Oh, it's nothing. I mean, it was a long time ago."

"Was it Bobby?" Holiday asked. "Is that what you were going to say? You didn't know I was here until after Bobby died?"

Michael hesitated. "Okay, look, this was a long time ago, and I'm not passing judgment or anything."

"Go on," Jaxson said.

"The night Bobby died, Dave, Beau, and I had been up in the cupola to take in the city and the fresh air. We were sharing a bottle of Jack Daniels and smoking some weed, nothing big. It was getting late, so the other two returned to the room, but I stayed up there a little longer. I was thinking about whether or not I should go to culinary school. Finally, I headed down. It must've been going on two in the morning. You come bounding up the steps and run smack into me."

Holiday thought back to that night. Waking up and finding Bobby dead in the bed in the Grand Mansion Suite, calling Tú, and Tú telling her to go to her room until she came from her grandmother's in Rock Hill. Was that when she ran into Michael?

She looked at Jaxson. "I don't remember that."

"You hit me pretty good. You would've hit the ground if I hadn't caught you."

"But I don't remember this," she said.

"I'm not surprised. As I understand from some of the scuttlebutt, you and Bobby were both drugged before he was killed. I'd be surprised if you remember anything after you woke up and found yourself in a room with a dead man."

It bothered Holiday that she couldn't remember running into Michael. Maybe the trauma of finding Bobby had caused her to block out some of the night. It was as if her mind kept secrets it didn't want her to know.

"What happened after Holiday ran into you?" Jaxson asked.

"She said something like 'take me home' or 'I want to go home' or maybe just 'go home.' I don't know. It was something like that. But you couldn't get your key to work. I took it and let you in. I tried to find out what had happened. I asked you if Bobby had done something to you, but you kept shaking your head and saying something about home."

Holiday slipped off her stool and stood, her arms

crossed. "I don't remember this! Why don't I remember this?"

"Then you did something else," Michael said. "You pulled out a syringe from your pocket—a hypodermic needle. You looked around, waving that needle, so I wasn't getting too close to you. But I asked you what you were doing. You were totally out of it. I knew you were either hyped up on adrenaline or on whatever had been in that needle. At the time, I thought maybe you and Bobby were using and trying to get rid of the evidence."

The door to the restaurant opened and closed, and Holiday jumped. She spun, but nobody had come in.

"You went to the armoire and ripped out a small piece of the trim in the back corner," Michael said. "I don't know how you did it with just your fingers. Probably the adrenaline. Maybe the trim was already loose. I don't know. You stuffed that hypo in the little crevice you'd created and shut the door. Afterward, I helped you get into bed with all your clothes on, and you fell asleep almost immediately. I shut the door and headed down to my room. That was the last time I saw you until last night at dinner."

Holiday closed her eyes and willed herself to remember anything Michael had just said, but she couldn't bring a scrap back. It was as if she'd blocked out that part of the night. But it made sense. She'd called Tú. And after that, according to Michael, she'd raced upstairs with the hypodermic needle and hidden it before Tú or anyone else could find it.

She'd hidden the murder weapon used to kill Bobby.

Jaxson looked at his watch, then shook Michael's hand. "I guess the two of us better get going. I appreciate your help on this."

"I hope I helped. We've needed someone to get to the bottom of this. First Bobby. Now Daily."

Jaxson and Holiday headed back across the lawn to the mansion and took the elevator to the fourth floor. The air was thick between them, the tension palpable. She wanted Jaxson to say something, but either he was refusing, or he was so lost in thought it wasn't occurring to him to let her know she was still his Watson.

Losing a whole segment of time had made her doubt so much of what she thought had happened that night. She wasn't sure she could trust herself to know what was real and what had been imagined. Had Bobby really died that night? Had she actually hidden the murder weapon? Had she even been at Wentworth Mansion twenty years ago? She wished there was some way to know.

At the door to Room 19, she stopped. There was a way.

"I need to check something," she said. "I'll be right back."

Jaxson placed a hand on her arm. "I don't know about you running around here alone..."

Holiday kissed him. "I'll be fine, dear. I'm just gonna go down to the front lobby and I'll be back up in a flash."

Jaxson nodded and slinked into the room, and Holiday took the grand staircase to the first floor, heading straight to the giant registry book by the front door. She flipped through the thin, oversized pages, a jumble of names, places, dates, and times.

"What did they do to me, to my memory, when they drugged me? Was I actually here that night?"

She looked down at the book and let her finger trace where she'd signed their names when they'd arrived the day before. Mr. Jaxson Bridgewater. Mrs. Holiday Trousseau

Bridgewater. And there was the little heart she'd drawn over both lines, uniting their names in love.

She let her finger scan down the page. There were the others. Dave and Payton. Beau. Tú. Michael. Where was Daily? She remembered Leonard had said Daily checked in the day before. She scanned back up the page, and there she was. Daily Southerleigh.

Oh, Daily. It was the last time you wrote your name.

But what about that night, twenty years earlier? Did she and Bobby sign in then? She couldn't remember. She was discovering that she couldn't remember much about that night.

She took a large section of the book and turned it back. Seven years ago. Thirteen years. Seventeen years. She was going back in time. The book was massive, and it was remarkable that the inn had used such a registry for so long. Only a place as charming, historic, and beautiful as Wentworth Mansion would have used the same registry for decades. Just like the actual keys that Jaxson found so intriguing. Just like the light classical music she could hear in the background.

She was now in the right part of the book. October. Twenty years ago. She skimmed down the page. And then she found it.

They had signed in on the day they'd arrived. Mr. Bobby Boudreaux and Miss Holiday Trousseau. She had been at Wentworth all those years ago.

She laughed. "I could've never married Bobby. Holiday Trousseau Boudreaux? Worst married name ever."

Her eyes fell on another name just a few lines below hers. All alone. In that familiar, unassuming script.

Daily Southerleigh

Daily had been at the inn that day. She'd signed in only a few hours after Holiday and Bobby.

Holiday slowly traced her friend's name. "You were here? But why? Were you mad at me because I stole Bobby from you?"

But she hadn't stolen Bobby. Daily had kicked Bobby to the curb. So why come to Charleston the same weekend as Holiday and Bobby?

She left the book and walked across the lobby to the parlor. The table lights gave the room a sleepy glow. She took in the beautiful marble fireplace on one end of the room and the old grandfather clock on the other, like guardsmen on duty. Holiday looked at her phone. It was ten until one. In a little over an hour, the clock would be correct again. What was that old saying about a broken clock being right twice daily?

Sometimes, all you get are two chances to be right.

Suddenly, she remembered Jaxson and how he hadn't said anything to her on the way to their room. She needed to get back to him. She needed to know if her husband still loved her and if he wanted to be married to her.

She chose the elevator, and as the carriage rose slowly, her thoughts drifted back to Daily. After breaking up with Bobby, Wentworth was the last place Daily should've been that weekend. And disappearing before dinner, twenty years later, was the last thing Daily should've done after inviting everyone back to the inn this weekend. Nothing about Daily made sense. She wanted to talk to Daily and understand.

When the elevator opened on the fourth floor, she went to the spiral staircase and fell to the floor in the same place where she'd found Daily's body.

And then she knew what Daily had done.

"You didn't come to Wentworth Mansion to stalk me the

night Bobby died," Holiday said. "You came here to save me."

She pulled herself up and took long strides back to the room.

She opened the door. "You're not going to believe—"

Jaxson was kneeling in front of the armoire. He'd removed the refrigerator that had been inside. His shirt was drenched with sweat. He stood and opened his hand. In it was a hypodermic needle.

"We have a problem," he said.

12

Jaxson carefully held the needle in one hand and wiped his brow with the other. He'd worked up a sweat removing the refrigerator from the armoire, then moving the oversized cabinet away from the wall so he could examine it more thoroughly. He'd cut several fingers, breaking through the molding on the inside of the armoire, and he was about to have to take his second shower in five hours. But that wasn't what was bothering him. His wife of only six months stood before him, her face ashen white as she stared at the old hypodermic syringe that he'd found buried in the crevice of the antique cabinet. And by the look on Holiday's face, he could tell she was as surprised as he was to see the needle after all the years it'd been hidden. But did that mean she didn't know it was there? Six months wasn't very long to know someone, and the evidence against her was mounting.

"Did I do that?" Holiday shuddered as she blinked at the syringe.

Jaxson placed the needle on the antique desk and lifted the fridge back into the armoire. "Maybe you did, but it still doesn't prove you killed Bobby. It wouldn't be the first time a crime victim hid the weapon. If you were in shock that night when you found Bobby's body, as I suspect you were, you could've done any number of things that wouldn't make sense to a rational mind."

He hoped that was all it had been.

"Oh, God, I just want to be done with all of this." Holiday slumped down on the edge of the bed and buried her face in her hands. "Maybe I am the one who killed Bobby, and I just don't remember."

Jaxson knelt beside her and pulled her close. "I think it's time we got some lunch."

She lowered her head to his shoulder. "Do you think I killed him?"

"Not a chance. Did you steal evidence and hide it that night?" Jaxson shrugged. "We need to keep putting the clues together and see where they lead."

"I hope they don't lead to me," she whispered.

Which was precisely what Jaxson was thinking. Holiday had said that Daily had a secret to share about Bobby's murder, a secret that would presumably lead to the killer. But Daily couldn't have known about the syringe because it was still hidden. What had Daily uncovered if it hadn't been the murder weapon?

Holiday lifted her face. "Daily was here. That night. Twenty years ago. She was here when Bobby was murdered."

Holiday told him about Daily's signature in the old registry.

Jaxson lay back on the bed, his arms outstretched above his head. "Why would she have come here that night?"

"You don't think Daily killed him, do you?" she asked. "Maybe she was so mad at him for the drugs that she followed him here and killed him. Maybe it was her way of protecting me."

Jaxson shook his head. "Doesn't fit. I mean, what kind of drugs are we even talking about? Pot? Coke? Did Daily's mother say?"

Holiday shook her head.

"You see what I mean? Coming here and keeping an eye on you, I can buy that. But if Daily killed Bobby, why would she stage an elaborate reunion just to figure out who did it after twenty years? I think we can safely rule out Daily as a suspect. There had to be another reason she would travel all this way that day when she knew her ex was with her best friend."

Holiday lay back and snuggled against Jaxson's shoulder. "I miss Daily. All those years, I thought she despised me. Why didn't she reach out to me?"

"Maybe she was angry at first. Maybe she needed some time to heal from all that had happened between her and Bobby and the two of you. Plus, she had her career to think of. Her art business and trying to piece together all that happened the night Bobby was killed. It's a lot for one person. It's also just kind of how it is sometimes. Some friends are just for a season in life."

"I missed so much time with her."

Jaxson kissed the top of her head. "Let's go to Peninsula Grill. I hear they make a mean coconut cake, and their biscuits are to die for."

Jaxson needed a change of scenery, and from the stress etched into the lines on Holiday's face, he suspected she did too. The walls of the murder investigation that had been thrust upon him had begun to close in, and the cool, fresh air and the bright sunshine would refresh them as much as a hearty meal at one of Charleston's most renowned restaurants. Finding the hypodermic needle had only raised more questions than it answered, answers that Holiday didn't have. Over lunch, though, he'd ask her questions she could answer, questions about her time with Bobby.

After a short ride down Wentworth Street and over to North Market courtesy of a rickshaw bicycle taxi Leonard had summoned, Jaxson and Holiday found themselves on the restaurant's covered cobblestone patio adjacent to Planters Inn Hotel, a warm plate of biscuits between them.

Jaxson looked around to see if anyone was within earshot. "Let's assume Daily came here to keep an eye on you. Was she afraid Bobby would seduce you into taking coke or crack or whatever it was with him?"

"She knew me better than that."

"Supposedly, Bobby was killed before he could explain what this big business opportunity was all about. But that's a lot of expense and effort for three guys to come to Charleston for a prospect they were unaware of. The whole thing sounds fishy."

"Speaking of fish, dear, I'll order the eight-ounce grilled salmon."

"We'll make it two. I don't want to fill up too much when we have a murder to solve."

"Do you think we can do it?"

He smiled at her. "We're gonna try, baby. What was the message Daily left for you on the mirror?"

"I still love you always. Replay the day," Holiday said.

"Exactly. That's what we need to do. We need to do the same things you and Bobby did that day. Something happened that Daily discovered, something that helped her figure out who killed him." He took the cloth napkin from his lap and the pen from his pocket and wrote down the number one on the napkin. "Okay, what was the first thing you did that day?"

"If I'm not mistaken, the first thing we did was take a carriage ride."

Jaxson jotted it down. "Okay, that's what we'll do first. Then what?"

"Fort Sumter." She smiled. "Guess you'll get to see it with me after all."

Jaxson made another note on the napkin. "What happened after Fort Sumter?"

Holiday shook her head. "That was pretty much it. That was all we had time for. He kept wanting to hurry up and get back."

"What was the big hurry? Do you think it was about this big business venture of his?"

"I don't know. He never said." Holiday folded her napkin in her lap. "What about Payton and Tú? Find out anything good?"

Jaxson filled her in on Payton's comments, then replayed Tú's version of the story that night and showed her the group photo he'd texted to himself.

Holiday held his phone to get a better look. "I remember that day. I bet I still have that photo on my phone." She sighed. "Those were the good days of the Crazy Eights."

The food was served, and the couple devoured every bite. Holiday ordered a slice of the restaurant's famous Ultimate Coconut Cake, which they also ate. Lunch over, the pair raced down Market and joined a group taking a carriage ride tour of old downtown Charleston. The driver guided the horse away from the curb, and the carriage ambled down the cobblestone road, taking a left on Church Street, a left on Broad, and a right onto East Bay past the colorful row of 18th- and 19th-century homes.

"I remember Rainbow Row!" Holiday exclaimed.

"Believe it or not, folks," their tour guide said, "the Charleston Harbor came right up to this road we're on. It wasn't until later that the Bay was filled in to make room for the buildings you see on the other side of the street. The residents used to live on the top floor and had businesses on the ground level."

"I just remembered something," Holiday said. "We didn't take the first available carriage that day. Bobby made us wait. He said the carriages take different routes, and he wanted the one that went past Rainbow Row."

"Did he say why?"

Holiday was quiet for a moment. "No, but it seemed like he wanted to see something, some building or house. He kept looking around and asking what street we were on." She snapped her fingers and stood. "It was a pineapple." Her eyes cut around to the buildings and sights passing them by. "It was a fountain. An old pineapple fountain."

Jaxson called out to the driver. "Is there a pineapple fountain around here?"

The driver pointed to his left. "It overlooks the Harbor. And the lady will need to take her seat."

"Bobby made the driver stop and let us out," Holiday said, "and that's where we went."

"We'd like to get off here," Jaxson called out to the driver.

The man looked at them curiously but pulled the horses and the carriage to a stop, and they hopped off. They raced across the street and down an alley until they reached a wide sidewalk on the edge of Charleston Harbor. Ahead was a three-tiered water fountain with a pineapple-shaped top.

"This is it." Holiday motioned to a bench. "He told me to sit here. Said he needed to talk to someone." She went around to the other side of the fountain, and Jaxson followed her. "He came over here, and a guy, probably in his thirties, short and round with wide black sunglasses, walked up to Bobby and handed him a white envelope. Then he left, and Bobby said he got us tickets to Fort Sumter. I was so confused. Bobby had said he'd wanted a wonderful romantic getaway with me, yet it was like he was trying to work something else into our weekend and wouldn't tell me what it was."

"Maybe it had to do with this business opportunity?" Jaxson took a step toward Holiday. "Wait. Don't turn around. Someone is watching. Just kiss me."

Holiday kissed him long and deeply.

Jaxson laughed. "Okay, that was more than I expected, but very convincing. Pull out your phone and take a selfie of us with the fountain in the background. A man in a gray hoodie and a Carolina Panthers hat is on the other side. Make sure he's in the picture when you take it. Go."

Holiday took the photo, and Jaxson pulled her closer.

"Excellent," he said. "Good work. Let's head back toward Bay Street."

When they'd returned to Rainbow Row, Jaxson stopped them. "That man, I'm pretty sure he was at the bar at Peninsula Grill. He followed us when we left. I didn't think much of it at the time. But there he was again at the fountain."

"What do you think he wants?"

"I don't know. Maybe we can use facial recognition to Google something about him when we get back."

Holiday took Jaxson's hand as they walked down East Bay Street. "Now what? Fort Sumter?"

"Yes, and it's a pretty good walk from here." Jaxson pointed to a stand of green electric bikes for rent. "Come on."

If the man in the photo were tailing them, that could

only mean one of two things. Either they had been made as easy marks by some local crook, and he was biding his time until he could rob another pair of out-of-towners, or, and this one made the most sense, one of the Crazy Eight suspects had a local accomplice. Jaxson hoped the man was just another low-life criminal. If he wasn't, Bobby's killer was getting nervous about Jaxson's investigation and was keeping tabs on them. Either way, they needed to shake their shadow.

They rented the electric bikes and pedaled north, parking them across the street from the Fort Sumter Visitor Center. Twenty minutes later, they boarded the ferry and were on the water. The boat was a split-level vessel with tables and benches below and rows of white plastic chairs above. The couple settled on the starboard side of the top deck. There was no sign of the man in the gray hoodie and Panthers ballcap.

Jaxson looked around. "I don't see our friend. He could be below. Maybe it was just a coincidence."

The boat docked, and Jaxson and Holiday followed the crowd of visitors down the gangway and into the old rock fort. Just one crumbling stone wall flanked the entire perimeter. Jaxson had seen enough photos of Sumter to know that at one time, the fort's walls had been two stories tall and consisted of barracks and other quarters where the soldiers lived and took their meals when not drilling or on duty. A large, black, and unattractive metal building called Battery Huger divided the fort in half. Partially underground, it was not originally part of the garrison. It had been added during the Spanish-American War, and it was to the top of the Huger that Jaxson wanted to go first to get a better layout of the stronghold.

"It's so pretty and peaceful here. I can't believe this is

where the first shots of the Civil War were fired," Holiday said as the two climbed the steps to the tallest point of the fort and stood by the flagpole. From there, they had a good view of the harbor and the cannons scattered around the edges of the walls.

They took the steps down the back of the Battery Huger, and Holiday stopped them alongside one of the wall's embrasures. "I remember now!"

"The hypodermic needle?" he asked.

"Bobby stopped here." She pointed to the wall, her eyes darting back and forth. "That day was like a treasure hunt for Bobby. He was going from cannon to cannon all along the wall on this side of the fort."

"He was looking for something," Jaxson said.

"It seemed that way, but I didn't ask him about it because I didn't want to annoy him. You had to be careful with Bobby sometimes. He would get defensive if you asked too many questions. He always took it as an affront that you didn't trust him. So I just let it go. Plus, I was still getting to know him. Maybe this was the way he sight-sees, you know? Like a man on a scavenger hunt."

Jaxson squeezed her hands. "The man you saw at the pineapple fountain probably told Bobby to come here, that something was waiting for him. Otherwise, you'd think Bobby would have come here first, considering he was so eager."

"What could he have been looking for?"

"Good question," Jaxson said. "Money? Drugs? A gun? Something shady he needed from the short round man. Maybe he came out here looking for something for this new business opportunity." Jaxson's phone buzzed. "It's a message from Beau. Says he has something I need."

"Should we head back to the ferry?" Holiday asked.

"Let's do."

The two began walking.

"Did Bobby ever find what he was looking for?" Jaxson asked.

"I don't know. He could tell I was tired of being dragged around like a kid at the grocery store, and he told me to go to the ferry. I waited, but he never came, so I headed back to the mansion alone. He showed up hours later. He said he'd gotten caught up in the fort's history and reading all the plaques, but I knew it was something else. That's when I told him I didn't think it was gonna work for the two of us."

"How did he take it? He'd just spent all this time and money taking you to the most beautiful inn in Charleston, and you broke up with him." Jaxson laughed. "His second break-up in a week!"

"Surprisingly, quite well. I was shocked but also relieved. That reminds me. We need to ask the other Crazy Eights about that woman claiming to be his wife the night he died. I wonder if anyone else saw her."

Jaxson pointed toward the bathroom on the second level of the Battery Huger. "I need to hit the head. You too?"

"Ew, I hate it when you say it that way." She rolled her eyes. "I'll just wait for you down here."

Jaxson ran up the steps of the old black building and into the restroom. A few minutes later, he was back and found Holiday standing near some of the crumbled-down walls of what had once been the fort's dining hall.

"He's here," said Holiday, her face ashen. "The man at the fountain. He came up to me."

Jaxson grabbed Holiday's hand. "Did he hurt you?"

She shook her head. "He asked how I was and if I liked Charleston, and I said I didn't know, and he laughed because we both knew that was a stupid answer. He said you and I should be careful in Charleston because many visitors get hurt here, and the sooner we return to Dallas, the better."

Jaxson surveyed the area around them but found no sign of the man. He could feel his heart pounding, and he clenched his fists. If he could find the man, he would flatten him.

Holiday pressed herself into Jaxson. "I'm so scared, dear. If he knows we're from Dallas, he probably already knows we're staying at Wentworth."

Jaxson pulled Holiday toward the ferry. "Come on. Let's get back to the mansion."

They boarded and took their seats on the upper deck. Jaxson took one final look at Fort Sumter as the boat pulled away from the wharf. The Carolina Panthers man stood before the entryway door of the old fort.

And he was waving at them.

13

From Fort Sumter and back to the mansion, Holiday had been nagged by something Jaxson had said to her inside the old fortress. It wasn't about the man following them, though she did find herself looking over her shoulder several times during their rickshaw ride across historic downtown. Instead, Jaxson had asked a question as they stood before the canons near the wall's embrasures, and she'd known then the question was bothering him for the same reason it had bothered her. She couldn't remember the answer.

The hypodermic needle?

He wanted her to remember taking the syringe to Room 19 after finding Bobby dead. But did it matter? Jaxson had even said it didn't prove she'd killed Bobby. Still, he wanted to know. The truth was, she was afraid to recall too much. She might remember something she'd been trying to forget. She might remember that she had taken it or, even worse, used it on Bobby.

But Daily had been right. The way to find Bobby's killer, and now Daily's killer, was by replaying the day, and that meant remembering how it had all gone down. Her grandmother had once said that thoughts had a way of untangling themselves as they passed over the lips and through the fingertips. As unpleasant as it would be, when they returned to their room, she would write it all down from beginning to end. Maybe she would remember something new. Perhaps she would remember the hypodermic needle.

She'd been thinking about that syringe as she and Jaxson climbed the steps of the grand staircase when she saw a large black man in a long yellow coat standing outside the door to their room. He lit up when he saw them and gave them a brilliant white smile. He was almost a foot taller than Jaxson, with mammoth arms and a high sheen on his shaved head. He shoved his thick hand forward, and Jaxson took it eagerly.

"Jax, my good friend." The man had a deep, melodic Jamaican accent. "It is wonderful to see you again. And this gorgeous woman must be your new wife. Only the best for you, my friend."

"Holiday, meet Christopher Belafonte. We worked at the same school for a while after college." He turned to Christopher. "Until you got too good for elementary and went to secondary."

"I found my niche," Christopher said. "Holiday, you are as lovely as everyone says."

Holiday felt her face warm. "I didn't know you had a friend coming to see us."

"I texted him on the ferry ride back from Fort Sumter when you went to get a drink." Jaxson patted Christopher on the shoulder. "By day, he's a principal at a high school outside Charleston. But this weekend, he's gonna be your bodyguard."

"Bodyguard?" A shudder ran down her spine. "Let's get inside the room to talk more privately."

They sat before the fireplace, and Jaxson gave Christopher the rundown of what had happened and their immediate plans for the investigation.

"I have to meet someone at Halls Chophouse in downtown Charleston," Jaxson said.

"Excellent food there," Christopher said. "And on Sundays, they have gospel music. We should go sometime."

"Will you keep an eye on Holiday while I'm gone?" Jaxson asked. "Hopefully, we won't have any stalkers, but, you know, just in case."

"This is why I'm here," Christopher said.

"I owe you one for keeping Holiday safe for me."

"It will be my pleasure, friend. And it will also be my pleasure for you to stay safe, too."

Holiday kissed Jaxson and closed the door behind him. Then she pulled the inn's stationery from the antique desk and wrote.

Saturday night at Halls Chophouse meant a couple of dozen people outside waiting to be called in. Soft piano music drifted onto the sidewalk. Everyone wore coats and sweaters to ward off the chilly breeze blowing down King Street. The owner glad-handed the eager guests and rewarded their patience with flutes of bubbly champagne. Jaxson checked in with the receptionist, and another hostess escorted him upstairs to a semi-circular table against the wall. The place was packed, a cacophony of colors, sounds, and textures, every table filled with the culinary delights for which Halls had become well-known.

Beau sat in the middle of the half-circle booth but slid to one side when Jaxson approached. His crutches leaned against the table.

There was only one reason why a man on crutches would want to meet a mile away from his room for an impromptu meeting. Beau knew a secret, and it benefited him to keep it that way. So why tell Jaxson? That's what Jaxson wanted to discover, along with Bobby's big business opportunity.

"How's the leg?" Jaxson asked.

"Improving, I suppose. I'll get a second opinion when I return to Dallas." Beau gave the room a suspicious appraisal. "You didn't...that is to say, you weren't followed?"

"No. I made sure of it. I switched rickshaws five times on the way over." Jaxson smirked. "Why are we here? I left Holiday back at the mansion. Couldn't we have just done this there?"

A tinge of fear stabbed at Jaxson. As far as Beau knew, Jaxson had just left Holiday alone. He checked his phone for any messages from Christopher and found none.

"Listen. Make fun of me if you want, but there's something you need to know, and I don't want anyone to find out I was the one who told you. Look. Everyone might've agreed they wanted you to investigate, but that was just a cover. We all want it to return to how it used to be. Your new wife included." He leaned closer to Jaxson. "If the killer was one of the Crazy Eights, they wouldn't hesitate to kill you. The more I talk to you, the more my own life is in danger as well."

"You think you're next?" Jaxson asked.

Beau grabbed a crutch and shook it. "You're not hearing me! For twenty years, it's been forgotten. But we all knew something that the police didn't."

The waiter approached them and asked what they wanted. Beau ordered a beer, and Jaxson a Diet Coke.

"What didn't the police know?" Jaxson asked when the waiter left.

Beau shook his head. "This weekend, Daily getting us all together like this...it should've never happened."

"What do you mean?"

"Bobby's death...*fait accompli.*"

Jaxson held up a hand. "Hold up. Are we talking about this weekend or the one twenty years ago? Which one shouldn't have happened?"

"Both. Bobby was a dead man."

"His murder was inevitable?"

"Destiny. We all wanted him dead. Me. Dave. Michael. Payton. Especially Payton. See, here's the thing...The Crazy Eights? Bobby didn't want to be involved in the whole friendship thing. For Bobby, everyone was a tool, leverage, a commodity that could be spent at his pleasure for his future. Every relationship was transactional. Tú was the one who invited him into our little cadre. She rued the day. We all did. I mean, it wasn't just her. We all agreed to it. The day we said yes to Bobby was when the Crazy Eights began to die. But we were all too nice, hoping he would change. We didn't realize we all felt the same until after Bobby was gone."

The waiter returned with the drinks and asked about their menu choices, but Beau waved him away.

Jaxson's mind flashed to a book by Agatha Christie. A train. A murderer. Twelve passengers.

"Let's back up," Jaxson said. "What did Bobby do to everyone?"

"Look, I'm trying to help you and Holiday." Beau took a swig of the beer. "You guys are newlyweds. You've got the rest of your lives ahead of you. Daily, she was obsessed with the whole thing. The day Bobby died was the day the rest of us were all set free. But for Daily..." He shook his head. "That day imprisoned her. It was a quest for her, you know, to show everyone she could figure out who killed her ex."

Beau had a point, in a way. Daily had moved to Charleston to open her studio. She'd spent the last twenty years uncovering who she thought had killed Bobby. Supposedly, she'd invited all of them to the mansion to reveal the killer.

Still, Bobby's death deserved some justice.

"Who do you think killed Bobby?" Jaxson asked.

He laughed. "Isn't it obvious?"

Jaxson shook his head.

"Daily did it herself."

Jaxson sat back, removed his hat, and ran his hands through his hair. "No. I don't see it. Why would she invite us here just to reveal that she was a murderer?"

Beau slapped the table, bringing Jaxson to a start and causing several guests to turn. He lowered his voice. "You didn't know Daily like the rest of us. Holiday didn't even know what Daily had become because they hadn't spoken in twenty years. Daily Southerleigh needed constant attention. She was like a bucket with a hole in it. Why do you think she never married? No man was ever good enough for her. She ran through friends like a stack of ones at a strip club. This whole weekend was her way of getting herself back on our radar."

Jaxson rubbed his forehead. "It just doesn't make sense, even if what you're saying is true. There are other ways to seek attention than confessing to murder to a group of old friends."

Beau shrugged. "These serial killers write notes to the press or taunt the police if they don't think someone is paying enough attention to them. Look at Zodiac. He toyed with the cops in San Francisco for years. Same thing with BTK. I'm telling you, Daily Southerleigh set this whole thing up to grab the spotlight. And you want to know something else? Since Daily was the killer, there was no killer to expose. She wasn't going to confess. She was going to spend the entire weekend digging up old bones."

"She knew things about you guys?" Jaxson asked.

"Of course, she knew things. We all know things about each other. We were close. Too close. But that doesn't mean we're out there spilling our guts." He pointed a finger at Jaxson. "Your wife included. We all have our secrets to hide."

Jaxson thought about the hypodermic needle. Had Holiday truly not remembered running into Michael and hiding the syringe? And what about the mirror on the wall? She hadn't acted shocked at all. She'd immediately suggested it'd been Tú who'd written the message.

Beau took another gulp of beer and set the glass hard on the table. "You and Holiday don't need this. What's done is done. If you ask me, Daily just did what the rest of us wanted to do. And then we all moved on and enjoyed our lives." He leaned into Jaxson and whispered. "We were all better without Bobby."

Daily had been at the mansion the night Bobby was killed. And she'd been unhappy with him just a few days before he and Holiday came to Wentworth. Still, it was hard to imagine Daily needing so much attention that she'd plan a weekend to drag it all back up and risk everything she'd built for herself in Charleston.

Jaxson placed both hands on the table. "What was the argument about the morning before Bobby died?"

Beau's mouth opened, but no words came out. He blinked several times at Jaxson. Then he took another sip of the beer, setting the glass down lightly. "What argument? I don't know what you're referring to."

Jaxson smiled. "There was an argument in Room 10 the morning before Bobby and Holiday went to Fort Sumter. Bobby said he'd gone upstairs to get his wallet, but instead, he'd ducked into the room you shared with Dave and Michael. I have a witness who puts Bobby in the room with you."

Beau let out a soft obscenity. "Okay, he was there. I may as well tell you since you'll ask Dave, too."

"You didn't mention Michael. He wasn't there?"

Beau shook his head. "He left. Went to look around downtown, as I recall."

Michael had been telling the truth.

"What did you guys argue about?"

Beau shrugged. "Can't remember for sure. But I know it had to do with Michael. Bobby didn't trust him. Said he'd be bad for business."

"Speaking of business, what was this big opportunity that brought you all to Charleston in the first place?"

Beau cleared his throat and scanned the room. "Never got a chance to ask."

"You guys argued about Michael being bad for business, but you never talked about what the business was?"

"Hey, what can I say? We were young and stupid. Bobby always had a plan. He had a certain way of doing things. It annoyed him if you asked too many questions."

"I've heard. You told me earlier today that Bobby was killed before you got a chance to talk to him. But that's not true. There was the argument."

"Bobby died before I got to talk to him about business. I

didn't lie." Beau looked at his watch. "Listen, I'm gonna have to go. Mainly, I wanted to offer you some free advice: just let it be. You don't want to end up like Daily."

The Crazy Eights were better without Bobby. Were they better without Daily, too? Would they be better without him and Holiday?

"Should I take that as a threat?"

Beau threw his hands up. "I'm just saying it would be better for everyone if you and Holiday dropped this investigation and let it be what it has been for two decades. Just another unsolved murder."

"Better for...everyone?"

"Better for Holiday."

"What do you know about Holiday from that night?"

Beau squirmed and looked at his watch. "I don't know, man, it's... You know, we were all young back then and made choices we wouldn't make today."

"What choice did Holiday make?"

Beau drew in a long breath. "Okay, fine. You're gonna find out sooner or later. But trust me, it's not something you're gonna want to know about your new wife."

"Try me."

***

It took all of ten minutes for Holiday to write down everything she remembered about finding Bobby murdered, but the exercise produced no new memories. She still couldn't remember hiding the hypodermic syringe in the armoire. She studied the cabinet across the room. Jaxson had laid the broken molding on the floor near one of its legs. The antique closet took on a sinister sneer as it seemed to consider Holiday's inept recollections. It could remember things Holiday couldn't, and she was thankful it couldn't talk.

She suddenly felt the urge to escape the room and all the past she couldn't remember. She suggested they go down to the library, and Christopher agreed if she stayed with him.

They settled into the library's green-and-taupe checkered high-back chairs.

Holiday frowned. "I'm worried about Jax. I hope he's okay."

Christopher gave her a wide, toothy smile and waved off her apprehension. "I'm quite sure your detective will be back very soon. I tell you what. Let's tell each other something about ourselves, which will help us pass the time."

Holiday crisscrossed her legs beneath her in the chair. "You go first."

"I grew up in Jamaica. Went to a small college in Arkansas. Got my first teaching assignment at the same school as Jaxson. It was an elementary school, and the principal hired me to teach kindergarten. Me. Teaching the smallest children in the school. I was like a giant sitting on those tiny chairs, teaching them to read. But we had fun. It was a bilingual class, which is how I suppose I got the job. I speak three languages. English, Spanish, and Jamaican Patois. From there, I worked at a middle school, teaching science and coaching football. After that, I went into administration and became a principal."

"What do you like to do? Watch movies? Travel? Concerts?"

"I like to play cards." He laughed. "I have a good poker face."

Holiday looked across the room. Board games and

puzzles were on the credenza above the computer. And Judith had been playing solitaire with a deck of cards.

She jumped up from her seat and crossed the room. "There are playing cards here. You could teach me how to play poker."

"Oh, I don't know. That might take some time," he said.

She sifted through the puzzles and games and found the old pack of Bicycle playing cards. She opened the box and poured the cards into her hand. "Okay, how do you play poker?"

Christopher hedged. "I don't think we have time for you to learn how to play poker. Plus, we have no chips. Maybe there is another game we could play."

It was the first game that came to mind, and she said it without thinking. "Okay, how about Crazy Eights?"

Holiday caught herself, and Christopher must've noticed.

"Are you okay?" he asked.

She gave him a nervous laugh and shook off the uneasy feeling. "I'm okay." She removed the joker from the deck and slipped it back inside the box. "You do know how to play Crazy Eights, right?"

He gave her a sheepish grin. "I only know how to play poker and solitaire."

"It's easy!" She shuffled the deck. "I'll deal each of us eight cards, and we'll take turns discarding a card on the pile in the middle. You discard when you have a card that is the same number or the same suit as the card on top. If you can't play a card, you draw until you can. The first player to play all his cards is the winner."

"I can do that. But I must warn you, I am a card shark."

"You haven't played me yet! Oh, one more thing..." Holiday dug through the cards until she found the eight of hearts and held it up facing Christopher. "All eights are wild, meaning you can play an eight on any number and on any suit. That's why they're crazy. And that means you want to hang on to them until you're ready to use them."

"Crazy Daily," he said.

Holiday squinted at Christopher. "What did you say?"

The bodyguard pointed to the card.

Holiday flipped the card around. In the middle of the card, in tiny script, were the words *Crazy Daily*. The two words had been crossed out, and beneath them, someone had written *Crazy Holiday*. A line had been drawn through those words as well. And at the very top of the card was one name: *Tú*. Tú's name had also been crossed out.

Holiday dropped the card to the floor and thumbed through the deck for the eight of spades. *Crazy Michael*. She dropped it to the floor and found the eight of diamonds. *Crazy Tú,* crossed out. Holiday's name was underneath, struck through with a single line. She dropped the card and continued searching. Only one more eight would be in the stack if the deck was complete. She found the eight of clubs and held it for Christopher to read.

"*Crazy Beau. Crazy Dave.*" He looked at Holiday. "What does that mean? Is it bad?"

Holiday dropped to the floor and spread the deck before her. "What about Payton and Bobby? I didn't see their names. There should be two more names."

She searched through the cards until she came to the king of hearts. Across the top was one word: *Me*. She set it aside and continued her search. Across the top of the king of diamonds was the same word: *Me*. She placed it with the other king, and when she found the remaining two kings, the spades and the clubs, she saw that someone had also written the word *Me* across them. No other cards were written on.

"Do you know these people?" Christopher asked.

"They were my closest friends during college. But one's missing."

Christopher picked up the box. "You put the joker in here."

He slipped the card out. Beneath the jester was one name. It wasn't Payton's. It was Holiday's.

Bobby had sent her a message from the grave.

Jaxson looked across the top floor of Halls Chophouse. The guests around him and Beau were lost in their laughter, conversations, and the food they were enjoying.

"Tell me what I don't want to know about Holiday," he said.

Beau took another drink of his beer. "What do you know about Bobby and Daily?"

"I know they were engaged until Daily called it off a few days before the trip to Charleston."

"Did you know that trip to Charleston was supposed to be a pre-marriage honeymoon for them?"

Jaxson shrugged. "Holiday said that Bobby decided to get out of town and invited her on a romantic weekend."

Beau guffawed and shook his head. "It's true, Daily called off the engagement. And Bobby indeed decided to turn the weekend into a business trip. But it's not true that he invited Holiday."

Jaxson furrowed his brows. "You're saying Holiday just chose to come with him?"

"I'm saying Holiday followed him. Just showed up unexpectedly here. You asked earlier why Bobby would bring Holiday along on a business trip that he had with three other guys. He wouldn't."

Holiday had fallen hard for Bobby, and she hadn't told her best friend she was going to Charleston with Bobby. Had she also not told Bobby?

"How do you know this?" Jaxson asked.

"Bobby told us. That's part of what the argument was about in that room. That and Michael not working out."

The waiter came over, and Beau waved him off again.

"We showed up a day after Bobby did, and when we arrived, we saw Holiday. We weren't even expecting Daily, so Holiday was a shock. Bobby said she followed him to Charleston, and he'd made up some story to her about wanting to spend the day together."

"Wait. Bobby told you Holiday followed him?" Jaxson closed his eyes and rubbed his forehead. He'd need to ask Holiday about this. "Did you know Daily was here too that weekend?"

"Yes. I saw Daily slip into her room just after we got here. Do I think she acted alone?" He shook his head.

"What's that supposed to mean?"

"Look at the evidence. Holiday follows Bobby here to the hotel, thinking he's alone. She gets inside his head and spends the day with him. Later that night, she gets into his bedroom. Then, Daily shows up. The next thing you know, Bobby is dead, Holiday's back upstairs, the murder weapon has disappeared, and so has Daily."

The group hadn't asked Jaxson to investigate the murders of Bobby and Daily because they wanted to root out a killer. They'd wanted him to piece together the evidence they already had.

"You think Holiday and Daily worked together to kill Bobby?" Jaxson asked.

Beau frowned. "Daily and Holiday hadn't spoken in twenty years. It would take a mighty big event to separate two friends who'd been as thick as they were. Follow the evidence, Jax. But if I were you, I'd let it be. Old bones don't like to be dug up."

14

———

Holiday studied the playing cards she'd spread across the desk in the library. Four eights, one from each suit, all with names. Four kings, one from each suit, all with the word *Me*. And the joker, with Holiday's name that wasn't crossed out. She was the most useless, ugliest card in the deck. She'd gone from the hearts to the diamonds to the joker. Her stock had diminished faster than a tray of petit fours at a bridal shower.

"Someone was assigning roles," said Christopher.

"But where is Payton's card?" Holiday sifted again through the scattered deck before her.

Christopher pointed to the four kings. "Perhaps it is safe to say that the one who assigned the cards is the one who gave himself the role of king."

"Bobby." It had to be. She picked up the kings. "Christopher, you're the card player. Do the four suits symbolize anything?"

"It's often said the diamond represents money, and the heart is love. The other two? Not so clear. Perhaps the club symbolizes military strength."

"A weapon for killing."

He nodded.

"And the spade?" she asked.

"A common working man? A digger of ditches?" He pointed to the kings. "If we take them at face value, this person, Bobby, suggests he is the king of all. Money, love, war, and work." He shrugged. "Perhaps I am overthinking. Maybe your friend was goofing around, just passing the time."

Holiday cringed at the suggestion that Bobby was a friend. The more she learned about him, the more she doubted she'd ever known him at all.

She considered the eight of hearts. First Tú, then Daily, then her.

Had Bobby been with Tú at one point? Who would he have gone to after Holiday had he lived?

"Your name is also crossed off on the eight of diamonds," Christopher said.

"I grew up in a wealthy family," Holiday said. "My father started a lucrative candy business."

"Perhaps this Bobby had assigned you the role of financial backer for this business opportunity that Jax spoke of?"

She'd been foolish with her infatuation with Bobby, telling him too much about herself in hopes of winning him over. Even then, she suspected it wasn't really her that Bobby had found particularly interesting. It was her father's business. Bobby was the only man ever to ask to see her father's quarterly P&Ls, and she'd foolishly obliged him, chalking up his unusual request to an inquisitive business mind.

"That makes sense," she said. "If I wasn't going to be his love interest, maybe he still wanted me for my money. But something made him change his mind again, and he crossed me off this one as well."

Christopher's voice was low. "Before you, it was Tú. Both of you for love and money. Both of you crossed off."

Holiday pointed to the eight of spades. "Michael was to be his working man in the business?"

"Possibly," Christopher said. "Dave and Beau on the eight of clubs. His military might? His strong men armed with weapons?"

Holiday grabbed Christopher's arm. "The day he was killed, Bobby met in Room 10 with these two, Dave and Beau, and the three of them argued."

"Perhaps he was meeting with the men who would do his bidding for him. Hitmen." Christopher let out a low whistle. "Who did Jaxson go meet at Halls Chophouse?"

"One of the hitmen."

J axson left the restaurant feeling even more unsettled about Bobby's murder. Beau had all but accused Daily of murdering Bobby with Holiday's help and had insinuated he'd been a more faithful friend to Holiday by not dredging up the past.

There was a lot to sort out, like when he was plotting his next mystery. The clues. The red herrings. The suspects. Only this one wasn't his story. It was a lot easier to solve a murder when he was planning it.

He thought about taking a rickshaw back to the inn, but walking in the cool evening air would clear his head. He was crossing Market Street when he saw the man in the Panthers hat. Did the man ever give up? Had he been at Halls Chophouse, too? Perhaps he'd seen him and Beau together. The man tried to duck inside a store doorway when Jaxson turned, but Jaxson had already seen him. Jaxson jogged to a rickshaw taxi on the opposite corner.

"Where to?" the lean young driver asked.

Jaxson didn't want to lead his tail back to Holiday and Christopher, and he wanted to follow up on something Leonard had mentioned when they'd checked into the inn.

"Have you ever heard of a place called Southerleigh Galleries or something like that?" Jaxson asked.

"Yeah," the kid called over his shoulder. "It's called Southerleigh's Fine Arts."

"Can you take me there?"

"Sure, man."

Daily's art gallery was on a small cobblestone street near the pineapple fountain. The building was a very unassuming, light pink, three-story structure with white awnings over the windows and door. The lights were off, but Jaxson tried the handle anyway. Locked. He walked around to the back and found another door. It, too, was locked. He cupped his hands around his eyes and peered through the window.

There was a desk, a computer, and some cabinets. There was also a round table covered in paperwork against one of the walls. Jaxson pulled away from the window and caught the briefest glimpse of a moving reflection behind him.

He spun, but not before the Carolina Panthers man plunged a needle into the side of his neck. Jaxson felt himself falling just before he blacked out.

<hr>

"Do you think Jaxson is in danger?" Holiday asked Christopher. "What if Beau is the one who killed

Bobby and Daily? Maybe he got tired of being Bobby's hitman. You don't think he'd do something to Jaxson?"

Christopher gave her a reassuring smile. "We have a saying in my country. 'My deh yah, yuh know.' It means 'everything is okay, you already know.' You can feel it in your heart. Your husband is okay. He is a wise and strong man. Now, let's get back to these cards. What else do you want to know?"

Holiday forced her mind away from Jaxson. "There are two things I'm still confused about," she said. "Where is Payton? And why is my name on the joker? I always remove the jokers and set them aside. I never understood why they're even there."

"That is an easy one," Christopher said. "In poker, the joker can be played as a wild card or seen as a 'bug,' which is a limited wild card. They sometimes trump other cards and complete flushes and straights. You keep a joker concealed in your hand until you know how and where you want to play it."

Holiday flashed back to that final day with Bobby. He had been trying to decide how to use her. He'd just been playing her all along.

The trip to Charleston. The promise of a romantic weekend at the mansion. The day of sightseeing. None of it was real. She'd been a wildcard. For sure, he needed money for this so-called start-up enterprise. But Bobby must have realized he needed something else from Holiday more than her money. He could've gotten the money from someone else. There was some other role for Holiday to play.

"It still confuses me why Payton is missing," she said. "Not that I want her in this weirdo deck of cards, but why is she the only one missing?"

"It's an old deck." Christopher pointed to the frayed

edges of several of the cards. "It's been here for decades. Perhaps she became a lost card."

Holiday's eyes lit up. "You're right. Let's see how many are missing."

They sorted the cards and put them in order by their suits. Every card was accounted for, except for one.

The queen of hearts.

"You don't suppose Bobby considered her his queen?" Holiday whispered. "She and Dave were already married by then."

"A man like this Bobby doesn't consider the feelings and thoughts of others. He takes what he wants and assigns where he wants. First Tú on the eight of hearts, then Daily... And then Payton? It makes sense. But there is one other thing to consider here."

Holiday looked up.

"Perhaps she was always there. Maybe he was concealing a queen while playing his heart. There is more than one way to view things."

Payton and Bobby were having an affair? Maybe. But what about the woman who told Judith she was Bobby's wife? Could Bobby and Payton have already been married when she supposedly married Dave?

Bobby had required collateral for Dave to participate in the new business, and Payton was pissed to learn the collateral was intimate photos of herself. Were they photos that Bobby had taken? If that were so, why would Payton want to be in a relationship with Bobby?

No, it had to be that Bobby considered Payton his queen or his future queen. It was ridiculous that he thought he could win her with blackmail, but that was Bobby.

Holiday's phone buzzed. "It's a text from Jaxson. He's in trouble!"

"How do you know? What did he say?"

Holiday swallowed hard. "He says it's urgent. He wants me to come to 4301 Gillion Street. But our safe word. *Incognito*. He didn't use it. If we want the other to do something unusual, we pair the request with the word *incognito*. It was his idea when we got married." Holiday began stuffing all the playing cards back into their box. "We have to find him."

"No worries, Miss Holiday, I will go find him. You go to your room and lock your door."

"I'm coming with you."

Christopher raised his hulking frame and brought his fingers together like praying hands. "Please, Holiday. Jaxson would not like this. He wants you safe here at the mansion."

Holiday put her hands on her hips. "Christopher, I appreciate your kindness, but I'm going to find my husband. Are you coming, too?"

"Mrs. Bridgewater, please don't do this to me," Christopher said. "I am your husband's friend. Either I go alone, or I don't go at all."

She knew he was right. Jaxson would not be happy if Christopher let her go, too. But she also knew it would be harder waiting than looking for Jaxson. Maybe if she read through the writing she'd done earlier, something else might have come to her mind from the night Bobby died. At least it would help her wait until she knew he was safe.

Holiday crossed her arms. "Okay, fine. But please hurry."

"I will," Christopher said, "but first, I will see you up to your room."

When Jaxson came to, he was lying on his side, his face smashed against the cold cement floor. He was gagged, and his feet were tied, his hands bound behind him. He had a massive headache. His vision was slightly blurred, but he could make out paintings on the wall, on a table, and leaning against the table on the floor.

Two black boots stood before him, and he lifted his eyes to see his assailant. He could only see as far as the man's waist, but it was enough to see that the man was wearing a gray hoodie.

"You should stick with writing mysteries, Jaxson Bridgewater. And your wife should be at home in Dallas selling candy."

The man had a thick Southern accent, similar to Leonard's.

Jaxson tried to ask the man who he was, but the gag mangled his words.

"You have questions. So do I. And I need answers from you regarding your investigation into this twenty-year-old matter at Wentworth. It is such a lovely establishment. Why bring all this drama to their doorstep? They don't need that. You don't need it. You should've never come, Mr. Bridgewater. Charleston is not the place for you. You should've left when I told your wife to leave, but instead, you came here. But I suspect we'll know soon enough what is to be done."

There was a rapping on the glass from the other room.

"That would be your lovely bride. We will also need to know what she knows. Excuse me while I get the door."

Jaxson prayed it wasn't Holiday. He'd left Christopher to keep watch over her, but Holiday wasn't the kind of woman to be deterred once she got her mind set on something. If she suddenly decided to locate Daily's gallery, would Christopher really be able to stop her?

Jaxson heard a loud crash and an explosion like a door coming off its hinges. It sounded like tables and chairs were being thrown in the other room. And then he heard the most-welcomed Jamaican accent he had ever heard.

"You are an evil man to try to trick a woman and bring her here," Christopher said. "Where is my friend Jaxson? Do you want me to break your arms?"

The man swore profusely. "Get off me!"

Christopher's response was nonverbal, but it must've hurt. The man screamed and begged Christopher to stop. The screaming ended, replaced by groans and heavy breathing.

"Now, we try again," Christopher said. "You answer my question, or I promise I will break it next time."

Jaxson tried yelling through the gag.

"Jax?" Christopher yelled. "Is that you?"

Jaxson let out another muffled cry.

"I'm coming, my friend. First, I need to take care of this bad man."

There was a loud smack followed by a deadening thud. A few minutes later, Christopher stood over Jaxson. He found a putty knife and leaned down behind Jaxson, freeing his hands and ankles. He pulled the gag down and cut it off. Then he helped Jaxson to his feet.

"Where's Holiday?" Jaxson asked.

"I left her safe and sound in your room at the mansion."

"Perfect. And thanks for rescuing me," Jaxson said. "We don't have much time. You may have told Holiday to stay put, but that doesn't mean she will. She probably won't. Plus, if someone passing by the gallery heard the commotion from you two, they will likely call the police. Let's see what this guy knows and see if there is anything in here to help us piece together what Daily was up to while we have the chance."

The other room was the front of Daily's gallery. The man who'd been following them all day still had on his gray hoodie, but his Carolina Panthers hat was across the room. He was balding, with a thin blond mustache and beard. He sat on the concrete floor, legs spread before him. His hands were tied behind him to the legs of a table. His feet were tied to the legs of a steel cabinet. And he was out cold.

Christopher smiled. "I had to knock him out so I could tie him up properly."

"I'm glad you and I are friends. Let's wake him up."

They found a small kitchenette in the back of the office, and Jaxson filled a large cup with water. Christopher dumped the water on the man's face, and he came to, sputtering and gasping for breath.

Jaxson nudged the man's leg with his foot. "You ready to do some talking now?"

"He will talk," Christopher said. "This man and I came to a quick understanding."

"Who are you?" Jaxson asked.

The man let out an obscenity, and Christopher gave him a quick kick in the side, causing him to wince and gasp for air.

"Our understanding," Christopher chided. "Don't forget. If you do, I will break your arm."

"Who are you?" Jaxson asked again.

"Latrelle Biggins."

"What do you do, Latrelle Biggins?"

"I'm a private investigator."

"Most private eyes don't go around incapacitating people with needles. What'd you give me anyway? Who sent you?"

The man bit his lip and looked away.

"Can I kick him again?" Christopher asked.

Jaxson wanted to laugh, but checked himself. "Maybe our new friend will play nice and tell us who hired him, and he can walk out of here with all his limbs in one piece. Otherwise, sure. And break his arm, too."

"Look," Biggins said. "It was just a little pentobarbital, not enough to kill you. I just wanted to knock you for a while." He squirmed in his binds. "I...don't know who I work for."

Christopher took a step forward.

"No! I swear," Biggins said. "Honest to God. Look, I'm just contract labor. I do what they tell me!"

"Who are 'they?'" Jaxson asked.

"I told you. I don't know. I get a text. I do the job. And they send me the money wirelessly. I've never met my employer."

"Does he go by a name?"

"Calls himself Ace. That's it. That's all I know. Ace told me to persuade you to leave Charleston. I tried to warn your wife nicely."

Jaxson took a step forward. "Don't ever talk to my wife again."

"Okay, okay. Relax. I was just doing my job, you know. Ace said I needed to persuade you to leave. It didn't work, so I followed you here."

Jaxson scanned the room for broken windows. "How did you get in here anyway? You have a key?"

Biggins closed his mouth and looked away.

"You want me to search him?" Christopher asked.

Biggins's eyes got wide. "I picked the lock, okay?"

Christopher pointed to the private eye. "We gonna catch and release this guy or call the cops?"

Jaxson looked at the paintings on the wall, vivid abstract

originals, each signed by Daily. She'd been an excellent artist. She'd also been able to locate the missing painting hanging in the lobby of the Wentworth Mansion. And she'd discovered something new about Bobby's murder. His killer? Had she found that, too?

The gallery was likely not where Daily would've kept notes on her investigation into Bobby's murder. Once the killer knew Daily was investigating, the gallery would be the first place they would search for anything she'd found. The place had to be so innocuous and inconspicuous that the evidence couldn't be seen in plain sight. It had to be the last place anyone would think to hide a smoking gun. There was only one place Jaxson could think of.

"We need to get back to the mansion," Jaxson said. "But first, let's give this place a quick once-over. Then we'll make the call. Once the police get here and arrest our prisoner, they'll make the gallery off-limits."

Christopher nudged Biggins. "You got that? Just sit there nice and quiet, and you can go to jail with both arms still working."

"And to think," Jaxson told Biggins, "this giant of a man used to teach kindergarten."

"Too bad I wasn't your teacher," said Christopher. "You would've learned a few things from me and wouldn't be tied up on the floor like this."

Christopher let out a big, thunderous laugh.

15

———

Sitting at the antique desk, Holiday read her written account of the weekend Bobby died. Even after the third reading, she was still unable to remember anything new. It hadn't helped that she couldn't keep her mind off of Jaxson. Every nefarious possibility had lodged into her thoughts. She stood and began to reorganize their room, her jewelry, and Jaxson's computer bag.

She was cleaning off the warning from the bathroom mirror when a faint knocking came from the hall. No peephole, so she leaned her ear against the door, but there wasn't the slightest sound. She dropped to her knees, but the crack under the door was too small.

Then came another slight rapping. Somebody knew she was there.

"Mrs. Bridgewater? It's me, dear. Judith Rainier. Mr. Leonard said I could find you in Room 19."

Holiday breathed a sigh of relief and swung open the door. Judith was alone.

"Won't you come in, Mrs. Rainier?" she said, opening the door wider.

Judith looked around as she shuffled in. She crossed the room with her cane and eased into the Queen Anne-style armchair.

"You and your husband have a lovely room," she said. "I wonder if you and Mr. Bridgewater will make this an annual trip, the same as my Arthur and I."

Without a murder? And people stalking us? And a twenty-year-old mystery? I could see that.

What had brought Judith up one floor to visit with Holiday? Was it that both women had waited to marry? Perhaps Judith was lonely and felt a kindred spirit in Holiday. It would have to wait if Judith wanted to share casual, heart-warming stories. With Jaxson in danger, Holiday would politely suggest they talk later.

"I love that you and Arthur had that tradition." Holiday took the chair next to Judith.

"Arthur and I called our trips honeymoons. We created photo albums of our trips and even had a small business card holder where we stored the cards from every restaurant we visited. We just never fell out of love with each other."

Holiday smiled. "That's so sweet. I will remember those ideas. What can I do for you, Mrs. Rainier?"

"There is something else I remembered about that night when Mr. Boudreaux was killed."

Holiday's phone rang. It was Jaxson's number. She held up a finger to pause their conversation.

"Hello?" She tried to make her voice hopeful, but it came out small and weak.

"It is I, my love," Jaxson said.

The heaviness drained from her chest. It had been so hard not hearing from him! "Jaxson! Are you okay?"

"Thanks to your bodyguard, I'm just fine. I'll catch you

up when I get back. We're at Daily's gallery. Are you locked up and safe?"

"Yes, dear. I'm in the room visiting with Mrs. Rainier again."

"Perfect. Stay there. Christopher and I will look around the gallery and then head back."

Holiday suddenly remembered the playing cards. "Ask Christopher to tell you what we found in the mansion's library. Bobby may have been playing me before he died. I'll show you the cards when you get back."

"Okay, baby, sounds good."

There was a long pause until Holiday finally asked, "Are you still there?"

"Yeah, I'm here. Listen, I think I know who killed Bobby and Daily. You need to stay locked up in that room because I don't want anything to happen to you, too. However, I need your help with one thing." He told her what he was thinking and reminded her to be careful. "Wentworth Mansion has a killer, you know."

"I'll be careful. I love you, dear." Holiday ended the call and turned back to Judith. "Okay, where were we, Mrs. Rainier? You remembered something about the day Bobby died?"

"Yes. It was that night. I remembered something else I thought you might want to know."

"What is it?"

Judith folded her hands in her lap. "About a half hour after Mr. Boudreaux's wife came looking for him, another young woman came by. By then, I'd moved from the sunroom to the parlor, and I must've fallen asleep on the settee. Arthur liked to retire early, and I've always been a night owl, so I stayed in the parlor to read for a while. Well, I'd fallen asleep while reading, and for whatever reason, I woke up. Suddenly, I saw her. She was standing by the grandfather clock. And she had the most confused look on her face."

"Who was it?" Holiday asked.

"Well, that's just it. I don't know. She was about your age then. Long blonde hair. She was mysterious and quite nervous, I must say. She kept looking around, the poor thing, almost as if someone were chasing her."

Daily? "She never gave her name?"

"Not one time. However, I must confess that the moment happened so quickly. I don't think I told her mine either."

"Did the woman say anything?"

"She asked me if I was dead, too!" Judith clasped her hands together and laughed. She had little crinkles in the corners of her eyes.

"That must've been quite a shock to you. What did you say to her?"

"That she startled me. And I remember thinking at the time that there were certainly a lot of young people running around this old inn. Wentworth Mansion is wonderfully quiet and peaceful, and it's not where a bunch of young singles still sowing their oats usually want to congregate. And yet, on that weekend, they seemed to be everywhere. And then, when I woke up, another one was staring at me from across the room."

"Why in the world did she wake you?"

"Well, you see, that's just it. She asked if I came here a lot. I told her I came with Arthur every year on this same weekend. She said I reminded her of her grandmother and asked if I would hold onto something for her and not tell anyone. She said it had to be kept a secret and that she would meet me here in one year to retrieve it."

"What did she want you to keep?"

Judith handed Holiday a small, bronze skeleton key on a simple silver chain. "Just this."

Holiday turned the key over in her fingers. It was no bigger than a couple of inches in length, the kind of key she'd seen in old movies often used for opening creepy rooms or safes behind pictures or padlocks on jail bars. "What's it for?"

"She didn't say, only that I must tell nobody I had it or that she would return for it. I could tell she was mixed up in something. I asked her if it involved a man, and when she said it did, I patted her hand and told her I would be back at the inn one year from that day."

What was so important about the key that Daily had asked Judith to keep it? Was she afraid it might get lost, or discovered, or stolen? No, it wasn't about the key. It was what it concealed. Daily was hiding a secret—if it was Daily.

"Did she ever come back?" Holiday handed the key to Judith.

"No. I had the key ready for her one year later, but she never arrived. I even asked the innkeeper if he knew about the young woman, and he didn't know either."

"You never saw her again?"

Judith's shoulders shuddered, and Holiday turned up the gas in the fireplace and offered Judith the blanket from the foot of the bed. Judith waved it away.

"I thought I had almost found her around five or so years ago. I was in the sunroom with Arthur and heard a woman's voice in the parlor. I swore to him that the woman I heard had given me her key. Arthur thought I was crazy, but I never forget a face or a voice."

"Was it her?"

Judith gave a slight shrug. "When I got up and crossed the room, she was gone. I asked Mr. Leonard about her. He said he'd been talking to a very famous artist who'd wanted to have a showing of her work here at the inn."

Holiday scooted forward in her seat. It had to be Daily. But what about the key? Had Daily forgotten about it after all these years? Did she no longer need it?

"A famous artist?" Judith said. "That didn't sound like the woman I met, so I figured Arthur was right, but I never told him that. Sweet Arthur. He always thought he was right."

Holiday reached for one of the woman's hands and held it firmly. "You miss him, don't you?"

"Every day, my dear. You never know how long you have with the most important love in your life."

A veil of silence fell over the room, and the two women sat side by side, watching the fire. Flickering orange, red, and yellow flames transfixed Holiday as they lapped deliciously at the air. Jaxson would soon be back from Daily's gallery. She wondered if they'd found anything that might help them understand what the artist had discovered. And she wondered if she had the strength to do what was next to see the mystery to the end.

Holiday pulled up a photo on her phone and handed it to Judith. It was the last photo of the Crazy Eights, everyone matching, standing at the top of Reunion Tower. "Is the young woman who gave you the key in this picture?"

Judith adjusted her glasses and leaned forward. "My dear, you are even more beautiful today than twenty years ago."

Holiday felt her face warm. "You are so sweet. Trust me, it takes a lot more work to keep it all going these days."

"Wait until you're my age. Then you'll know just how much work it takes." Judith pointed to Daily. "There she is. That's the girl with the key."

Even though she had expected this response, Holiday felt her heart skip. "That's Daily. Are you sure that's the woman who gave you the key?"

"Daily," Judith repeated as though she were trying the name on for the first time. "It's a pretty name. All these years, I had never known it. Oh, yes, that's her. I never forget a face or a voice. Do you still know her? You could tell her I still have her key."

Judith didn't know. She hadn't realized.

"I'm sorry, Judith," Holiday said. "The woman who was found at the bottom of the spiral staircase last night—it was Daily."

The air went out of Judith. "I...I had no idea."

"Daily was an artist here in Charleston. That was probably her voice you heard several years ago."

"It would seem that many of the young people in your picture were at the dinner table with you the other night."

"Daily had invited us all here to talk about Bobby's death."

"Yes. But I didn't see Daily with you."

"She was supposed to be there. I found out at the last second that she wasn't going to make it, and that's why I ran out so quickly. I wanted to talk to her."

Judith nodded as she studied the photo. "There is someone else in this photo that I didn't see the other night either."

Holiday joined Judith beside her chair. "You do? Which one? The rest were there."

"This one." Judith pointed to Tú. "She wasn't there."

"Actually, she was," Holiday explained. "She was the one with the black bucket hat and mask."

"I remember her from that night also, the night Mr. Boudreaux died."

Holiday nodded. "You might've seen her with me. We… we were up kind of late."

Judith shook her head. "Oh, no, dear. I don't remember the two of you together. I remember her being alone. She was all alone when she spoke to me that night."

"She spoke to you? What did she say?"

"She's the one who asked me where Mr. Boudreaux's room was. She's the one who told me she was his wife."

<hr>

Jaxson and Christopher dug around in Daily's office for twenty minutes, their prisoner tied down in the gallery's front room. As suspected, their search had yielded nothing regarding Bobby's death. Jaxson checked the time. They needed to get back to the inn. They'd left Holiday for too long as it was, and, as he'd explained to Holiday, it was just about time to assemble everyone in the parlor. He didn't have a motive for the killing, not yet, but he was almost certain who'd killed Daily. With a bit of luck, he might be able to prove it, too.

"Does a bill of sale for a painting to a collector in Germany mean anything?" Christopher called out.

Jaxson closed a cabinet he'd been rifling through. "Doesn't to me. Daily probably had collectors around the world."

"Hey!" Biggins yelled from the front room. "This rope is cutting into my wrists!"

Christopher stomped to the doorway of the office. "You should've considered that before you jumped my friend."

They continued to plunder the office, and Christopher told him about the playing cards he and Holiday had discovered. As he spoke, a paper in a plain manila folder at the bottom of a desk drawer caught Jaxson's interest.

"Check this out." Jaxson held the document in his hand beneath the desk's lamp. "It's a lease agreement for a second gallery location in Rock Hill signed by Michael and Daily."

"Rock Hill. That's nearly three hours from here," Christopher said.

"Looks like Michael was going to lease space from Daily."

"You know this Michael?"

"He's one of our suspects." He folded the document and slipped it into his coat pocket. "Probably doesn't mean anything, but I want to ask him about it anyway."

There was a loud splintering in the front room. When they rushed in, Biggins hurled a chair that struck Christopher on the head and glanced off Jaxson's shoulder. They stumbled backward, and Biggins threw himself toward the front door and escaped into the street.

"There goes our prisoner." Jaxson grimaced as he touched his shoulder. "You okay?"

Christopher wiped at a cut across his brow. "I'll live, but now I have unfinished business with that man."

"Let's get you something for that nasty cut."

Jaxson found a first aid kit in Daily's office and patched him up. "We need to get back to the inn and check on Holiday. I don't want Biggins showing up there without us."

His phone buzzed. An unknown number, but he answered anyway.

"Jaxson? It's Dave, Payton's husband. Listen...I uh...that is, we want to talk to you. There's something you need to know about the day Bobby died."

"How'd you get my number?"

"Leonard gave it to me. I told him it was urgent."

"I can be back at the mansion in thirty minutes."

"It can't be here. It's too dangerous."

"Where?" He thought he heard a whispered argument. The happiest couple in the world wasn't getting along so well.

"Battery Park. One hour. In the gazebo."

"No way. How do I know this isn't a trap? Just go somewhere private and call me."

"Hey, man, I'm sorry, but this really should be said face to face."

Jaxson rolled his eyes. If this were one of his books, he would never let a character say yes to a meeting in a situation like this. It would be a setup, or the people his detective was meeting would be killed before they could tell him the big secret.

It was already dark, and Holiday was still alone at the inn. But something had changed Dave's mind about talking. He and Payton knew something she'd been afraid to tell Jaxson that morning. Something Dave had wanted kept hidden.

"Okay, fine, but an hour is too long. I'll meet you there in thirty minutes."

"Great. Seven-fifteen," said Dave, and he ended the call.

"I'm pretty sure I know what happened to Bobby, and maybe even Daily," Jaxson said to Christopher, "but I have two more people to talk to. Then I'll know for sure. And if I'm right, we'll wrap this case up tonight. Can you get back to the inn? I've got to head to Battery Park. I'll meet you back in the room as soon as I'm done."

Christopher nodded, and they set off in different directions.

16

That ceiling looks like our wedding cake.

Holiday stood by the old grandfather clock in the parlor and tried to imagine Daily in the same place that night, watching Mrs. Rainier asleep on the settee. What had she been up to?

Daily had discovered something horrifying that night, twenty years ago. Now, two decades later, she'd come to the old inn again, this time armed with the truth, ready to expose one of their friends as a killer. The intervening years had given Daily clarity.

Or maybe it wasn't that way at all.

Maybe she had just wanted to get the whole gang back together. Maybe Daily had fallen accidentally on the staircase and died, just as the police had suggested. A tragic twist of fate to die on the same day as her former lover. Just a terrible coincidence.

Had Tú been Bobby's wife? Bobby had been engaged to Daily, and Tú would've known this. Holiday had promised Jaxson she'd be safe, but she had to know if what Judith had said was true.

As soon as Mrs. Rainier left, Holiday called Tú, who agreed to talk with her in the parlor. The elevator was across from their door, and she'd taken it straight down to the main floor and gone directly into the parlor. She was probably safer there than she was in her room alone. Besides, Leonard was working in the lobby around the corner.

Tú entered the parlor from the sunroom. She wore a black, long-sleeve turtleneck dress that covered her boots. As she entered the room, she removed her hat but left her mask on. Her eyes were smiling—at least, Holiday thought they were smiling.

"Holiday!" Tú sang out. "Brr. It's so chilly out there."

"Thank you for talking with me, sweet friend," Holiday said.

Holiday wondered if her words rang as hollow to Tú as they did to herself. Could she sense Holiday's uneasiness?

Tú settled into the chair next to Holiday. "What did you want to talk about?"

Holiday leveled her eyes on Tú. "Were you and Bobby married?"

***

Jaxson hoofed it halfway to Battery Park before coming upon a rickshaw willing to give him a ride the rest of the way.

Try as he might, he couldn't imagine what Dave and Payton wanted to see him about. As the park loomed ahead in the darkening night, the driver carried on about how George Washington had had a house nearby and how native Charlestonians call the area The Battery. The yellow streetlights along the park's perimeter offered little compensation to visitors navigating the pebbled paths for the first time. A chilly breeze blew across the peninsula from the Charleston Harbor, and Jaxson turned up the collar on his coat. When they arrived at the gazebo, Jaxson paid the young man and waited for Dave and Payton.

Tú blinked several times. "Yes. We were."

While Holiday had hoped Tú would tell her the truth, her jaw still hit the floor. "I don't understand. Were you keeping it a secret?"

Tú shrugged. "We had to. My father wouldn't have paid my tuition if he had known I was married. I was in law school by then and couldn't afford it on my own."

"Did you think one of us would rat you out to him? We were your friends. Why didn't you trust us?"

"I did trust you, but I couldn't take the risk. My father always said the moment I got married, I'd be somebody else's problem. That's one of the nicest things he ever said to me. My father had a way with words."

"But...when did you guys get married?" Holiday asked.

"Bobby and I met, fell in love, and married before we ever met you. After we all began hanging out and I saw Dave and Payton, I wanted Bobby with me too, so I invited him into the group, and you all agreed."

Holiday shook her head. "I still don't understand. Bobby was engaged to Daily. And then he tried to date me. And all that time, he was married to you?"

Tú winced. "Technically, yes. But we were separated and headed for a divorce when he started dating Daily." She rolled her eyes. "Suffice it to say, he wasn't what I thought he would be."

"What did you think he would be?"

Tú arched one brow. "What does every woman want? To be the center of her lover's life. To be loved completely. To be thought of first and not last. I thought he would be the man who made my dreams come true, but he turned out to be the biggest mistake of my life. I'd already served him with divorce papers by the time he was telling everyone he was engaged to Daily."

"But why not tell Daily, me, all of us, what was happening?" Holiday cocked her head at Tú. "Even if your father had found out...How could you just let Daily think her relationship with him was healthy?"

Tú raised a finger at Holiday and narrowed her eyes, "Hold on. Before judging me, remember that you're the one who ran off with the man you thought she'd just been engaged to. You're no angel yourself, missy."

Tú's words stung, but they were true. Holiday had been fully aware that going to Charleston with Bobby might jeopardize her relationship with Daily. And yet, she had.

She and Tú had both been young and immature. And selfish.

Holiday stared into the fireplace on the other side of the room. It felt good to let her eyes escape into the flames and, for a moment, pretend none of it was happening.

"Listen, Holiday, I'm not blaming you. Remember, I was the one who came to you and helped you get out of that mess that night. I was your alibi. When the police asked me about you, I told them you and I were together all night in your room."

Holiday pulled her eyes from the fireplace. "Did they know you and Bobby were married?"

Tú nodded. "I told them straight up that he was my husband but that you and I shared a bed that night alone."

"Shared a bed? You made it sound like we were lovers?"

"I let them think what they wanted." She shrugged it off. "Hey, would I do it all again like that? No. The cops could have thought you and I killed him together to get rid of an inconvenient husband. Thank God they didn't. We were all so young then. As they say, hindsight is twenty-twenty. I should have told you and Daily that our divorce wasn't quite finalized, but we hadn't even told you we were married in the first place. What was I going to do? 'Oh, gang, Bobby and I have been married this whole time, and now we're divorced!' That would've been so lame."

Holiday leaned over, resting her elbows on her knees, her head in her hands. "I'm still having a hard time getting past the fact that you just let Daily and me think that Bobby was single."

"I let you two find out what I already knew: Bobby Boudreaux wasn't worth the time it took to say his name." She crossed her legs, a smug smile spreading over her lips. "And you did. You both dumped him. You both figured it out much faster than I did."

Tú was right. They had figured it out. Still, if Tú had said something, Holiday wouldn't have been at the mansion the night Bobby was killed, and Daily would still be alive.

Leonard stepped around the corner, his hands clasped together. "Mrs. Bridgewater? I'm sorry to disturb you, but a detective is here. He would like to speak with you."

Holiday turned to Tú. "I guess they have more questions about Daily. Wait, should I get a lawyer? You went to law school. Maybe you should come with me."

"I'm sure it's just routine. Plus, I never finished my degree." Tú patted Holiday's knee. "Hey, I'm sorry for not telling you about me and Bobby. It was dumb not to, and I should've."

Holiday nodded, but she was barely listening. She wondered about the detective and what he would say.

They stood and hugged. Holiday slipped around the corner where a tall, dark-haired man in a blue coat and tie flipped open a wallet, revealing a gold badge. "Detective Larry Wright with Charleston P.D." He looked at Leonard. "Is there someplace private for us to talk?"

"You may take the elevator or the stairs behind it to the conference room below."

"What's this about?" Holiday asked. Her heart was pounding. Where was Jaxson? "Do you have more questions about the night Daily died?"

Tú stood by the elevator. She was watching them and listening.

Detective Wright shook his head. "No ma'am. It's not about your friend, Daily. It's about Bobby Boudreaux. Evidence has come to light that contradicts your statement to the police that night. You were in the room with Mr. Boudreaux the night he was murdered."

The detective's stern eyes bore holes through Holiday. It was like standing before Marcus Emilian Trousseau when he'd had one of his unpleasant business days. Holiday shuddered as she stared at the detective and swallowed the lump in her throat.

"Is this true, Mrs. Bridgewater?"

Holiday nodded and tried hard not to cry.

The detective pointed toward the elevator. "We need to talk."

Twelve minutes past seven, a yellow taxi pulled up on Battery Street across from the old gazebo. Dave and Payton exited the car and took the pebbled walkway under the yellow beam of a streetlamp. They weren't holding hands. Her arms were folded across her chest, and she was two steps ahead of Dave. Jaxson wondered which one of them had had the idea of calling.

Dave nodded at Jaxson, and they took a seat in the gazebo.

"I'm sorry," Dave said, "about what I said to you this morning. Payton and I had a long conversation about this, and we..."

"You," she snapped.

"*I* should've been more forthcoming. I was out of line. Sorry for being a jerk. It's just...we thought this would never come up again."

And yet it had, like an old bone, long ago buried, somehow finding its way to the surface. Every member of the Crazy Eights had held a secret, and keeping that secret had become more critical than finding Bobby's killer, even for Holiday.

Jaxson eyed the couple. "What is it you wanted to talk about?"

"It's about Bobby," Dave said. "It's about this business venture of his you've—."

"Bobby was dealing," Payton said.

And there it was. Daily hadn't just found Bobby using. He'd been selling, too. Daily must've known this. She'd broken off the engagement, ready to move on with her life. Then Holiday went to Charleston with Bobby, which changed everything for Daily. She had gone to Charleston, too. She had to protect Holiday from a drug dealer with a plan.

Jaxson looked from Payton's face to Dave's. "Bobby sold in college?"

Dave closed his eyes. "And so did we."

"He doesn't mean me and him," Payton said. "He means him and Beau."

"What were you selling with Bobby?"

"We were selling *for* Bobby," Dave said. "Ecstasy. Crack. Heroin. Meth. A lot of meth and ecstasy. It's how we were able to afford school. My parents' money ran out, which was hard on Payton, too. Suddenly, here's Bobby. One day, he asked if I wanted to make some real money fast. He had a whole system, and all he needed were the hands to get the drugs from his distributor to his customers. I agreed to do it just one time, but the money was so easy that I knew I'd found a way to stay in school. I told myself I would only do it until I graduated. After that, I was out."

Jaxson's phone buzzed, but he ignored it. "But you didn't get out."

"Neither did Beau. The money was too good. Additionally, I had to consider graduate school. I figured I'd stay in it a little longer, you know, just to get through those last semesters."

"And you knew about all this?" Jaxson asked Payton.

She nodded.

"Who else was selling? Just you and Beau?"

"And Michael," Dave said, "although he was the last one in the group and didn't sell as much as Beau and I."

"Bobby didn't trust Michael." Payton pushed back the hair from her face. "Said he was a narc."

"An informant?"

"An undercover cop," Dave said. "Beau and I didn't believe it."

"Is that what the argument was about the day Bobby died?"

"Bobby wanted..." Dave started.

"Bobby wanted Michael dead," Payton said.

Jaxson looked in the distance toward the harbor. It was too dark now to make out much beyond the park, and he wondered if it was possible to see Fort Sumter from the gazebo during the day. Everything always became more evident in the light.

"Did he say who he wanted to do it?" Jaxson asked.

"Tell him," Payton said to Dave. "You're the one."

Dave stood and walked to the other side of the gazebo, his back to Jaxson as he leaned against the balustrade. He let out a sigh as he looked up into the inky sky. It was several moments before he replied. "Listen. I swear I wasn't going to go through with it. He said we were his right-hand men, and as we enlarged the operation, he wanted to know he could count on us for anything. He wanted to be sure of our loyalty, he said."

Again, Jaxson's phone buzzed, and this time, he took it out of his coat pocket and set it on the bench upside down.

"And that's what the argument was about?" Jaxson asked. "Killing Michael?"

"Michael had gone someplace, and Bobby came busting into our room and said it had to be done that day. He just said to make it look like an accident, like he'd fallen down the stairs coming from the cupola. But I swear I wouldn't have done it."

"I don't understand," said Jaxson. "Was the trip to Charleston about selling drugs or killing Michael?"

"It was both," Dave said, turning around. "Bobby wasn't too high on Michael from the beginning. Michael had come to Bobby wanting to sell, not vice versa, and that got Bobby nervous, like Michael was with the police."

"And was he?" Jaxson asked.

Dave shrugged. "We never knew. We found Bobby dead before we could kill Michael, so you know, that was that."

Bobby had wanted to kill Michael. Had Michael found out and killed him first? If he didn't know, had someone else killed Bobby to protect Michael?

"You found Bobby dead?" Jaxson asked.

Dave nodded. "The plan was for Beau and me to tell Michael that Bobby had a meeting in the Grand Mansion Suite. We would get him in there and kill him or tell him we had to go up to the cupola or something. I don't know. Then Bobby would move back upstairs to the first room he and Holiday had. The room you have now."

"Room 19."

"Right. But when we got there, we found Bobby dead on the bed, and Holiday passed out in a chair. We got out of there as fast as we could. The three of us went back to our room, packed up, and left. We were gone before sunrise."

"Did you ever tell Michael that Bobby had wanted the two of you to kill him?"

Dave shook his head. "We just wanted to return to Dallas and pretend the whole thing never happened. We never talked about it again until Daily got us all here. And we all knew what she was doing."

"And what was that?" Jaxson asked.

"She'd finally figured out who'd killed Bobby. We knew from the moment she'd moved to Charleston that she was going to investigate his murder. But none of us ever believed she would put it together."

"Who do you think killed Bobby?"

"I just don't know." Dave looked at Payton. "We've talked

about it occasionally, and neither of us can figure it out. So, we came to see what Daily had to say."

"Who do you think killed Daily?" Jaxson asked.

"Oh, that's easy," Dave said. "It had to be the same person who killed Bobby. And they made it look just like the accident that Bobby had originally wanted for Michael."

"There's one thing I'm still confused about," Jaxson said. "Why bring Holiday? From what you've said, she had no part in the dealing. Wouldn't she just be a witness to all the shade being thrown around that day? Why was she even in the room the night you guys were supposed to kill Michael?"

"Don't you see?" Payton asked.

Jaxson stared at the couple. If Holiday had invited herself to Charleston, as Beau said, Bobby would've been scrambling to do something with Holiday, keep her occupied, out of his hair, and out of the way of his drug business. But then, why invite her to his room when he planned to kill Michael there?

"Holiday was the patsy," Dave said. "She was the one Bobby had chosen to take the fall for Michael's death."

"His whole reason for bringing her to Charleston," Payton said, "was to set her up for murder."

Jaxson crossed his arms and looked back out over the harbor. "So, Holiday didn't just follow him? It was his idea from the beginning of that trip to frame her for Michael's murder?"

"At first it was going to be Daily," Dave said. "But when she dumped him, he turned to Holiday. He just needed someone to take the fall. He didn't much care who it was. When he entered our room that morning, Bobby said he'd have Holiday in the Grand Mansion Suite later that night. He wanted to get her drunk. He wanted to sleep with her.

And the next morning, when she came to, she'd find a very dead Michael in bed with her."

"But his plan backfired," Payton said. "Someone killed Bobby first, and when Holiday came to, it was Bobby she found dead in bed, not Michael."

"Beau said Holiday followed Bobby to Charleston," Jaxson said.

Dave nodded. "That's what Bobby told us that day in Room 10. Beau might've believed him, but I knew it was a lie."

Jaxson's phone buzzed again, and he picked it up this time. He had three missed calls from Christopher.

Jaxson called him back, putting the phone on speaker for Dave and Payton. "What's going on? Is everything okay?"

Christopher's voice was loud and crisp. "It's about Holiday."

Jaxson stood. "What about Holiday? Where is she?" He could hear yelling in the background. "Where are you? Who are all those people?"

"I'm in the parlor with her friends. But I can't find Holiday."

"You can't find her? She's not in our room? She said she would be there."

Jaxson heard everyone talking over each other.

"Jax, hold on." Christopher spoke to the others. "You haven't seen her? What about you? Wait. When was the last time you saw her? I'm Christopher. I'm Jaxson's friend. She was in her room, and now she's gone."

Jaxson yelled into the phone. "Christopher? Christopher! What's going on? Where is Holiday?"

"I'm sorry, Jax," Christopher's voice was low and sorrowful. "I have searched this hotel high and low, and I'm certain of one thing. Your wife is not here."

17

Holiday viewed the small, dark, frigid space around her, a tiny room no bigger than the powder bath in their home. Louvers atop one wall allowed only a small amount of light to seep through. She could scream, but she doubted anyone would hear. She sat in the inky darkness and wondered what would come next. A shiver ran down her spine. She couldn't tell if she was shaking from the cold or her nerves. Either way, her teeth rattled in her head.

The man who'd claimed to be a police detective had taken her there. He had grabbed her arm, his large hand wrapping itself around her bicep. And though he'd been firm, he hadn't hurt her. Thankfully, he'd given her a couple of blankets, and she'd wrapped herself up like a burrito.

Was Jaxson back at the inn? How long before the others would realize she was missing? Maybe they already knew.

She peered at letters scrawled on one of the rustic wall planks. It was hard to make out the characters. If only she had a little more light. She stared until her eyes adjusted enough that a few letters started to come through. There was an S and a Y and a...

In a flash, the words were there. They seemed to glow in the darkness.

She wasn't the first to be tucked away in the small, frozen cell.

Twenty-four hours earlier, another had sat where she was.

She whispered the words aloud.

"Daily Southerleigh."

<hr>

Jaxson looked around the crowded parlor. They were all there. Michael. Beau. Tú. Dave, Payton, and Christopher. Listening. Waiting. Silent eyes watching, wanting to know what they should do. It was up to Jaxson. They had charged him with finding a murderer. Now, they were waiting for him to tell them how to find the next victim. He would guide them until they found Holiday.

Jaxson turned to Christopher. "You've looked everywhere?"

Christopher was panting hard. "I've been up and down the stairs. I've looked everywhere."

Jaxson held up his phone with a photo he'd been sent. It was Holiday sitting alone in a dark room. The flash had caused her to grimace and turn her face.

"There was a message, too," Jaxson said. "Stay by the phone. No police."

Payton wrung her hands as though she might shake the fear loose. "I can't believe this is happening."

Dave put his arm around her shoulders, and she nuzzled her head against his chest.

Michael eased up alongside Jaxson. "What can I do?"

"Let's fan out and search the grounds. According to

Leonard, she was last seen going to the ground floor. She was probably taken out the back door. Look for any evidence outside that might indicate which way they went. Knowing Holiday, there's a good chance she dropped something that would give us a clue."

Michael nodded and turned to go, but Jaxson grabbed his arm. "Can I ask you something? It's an odd question, particularly right now, but I don't know who to trust in this house. Holiday's missing, and I need to be able to trust one of you."

Michael cut his eyes around and lowered his voice. "Yeah, sure, man. What is it?"

Jaxson nodded at Christopher, who began organizing the other four in their outdoor search for Holiday.

Jaxson and Michael crossed the parlor into the sunroom and stood by the back door.

"Were you working as a narcotics officer when you all were in college?" Jaxson asked.

The question seemed to catch Michael by surprise. He pressed his lips together. "I was."

"You were working undercover in the Crazy Eights to bust Bobby?"

Michael nodded again. "We didn't know at first who in the group was selling, but we suspected Bobby. I managed to join the group. The next thing I know, Bobby is recruiting me, Beau, and Dave to sell for him."

"You were working for Dallas PD?"

"My cover was a student at SMU. We knew that many drug deals on campus originated from a single source. I began asking around, and my investigation led me to the Crazy Eights. At first, I thought they were all in on it, but soon realized it was Bobby, Beau, and Dave."

"Once you knew he was the ringleader, why not just bust him?"

"We weren't after Bobby. We wanted Bobby's dummy man."

"Dummy man?"

"The supplier. Bobby was just the middleman. The supplier was supplying many dealers in Dallas, both on and off campus. We thought if we could follow Bobby far enough, he'd lead us to the source, and we could cut off the head of the snake. Those guys were organized, and they were moving the stuff fast."

"Did you know there had been a plan to kill you?" Jaxson asked.

Michael scoffed. "No, but I'm not surprised. I knew my life was in danger the whole time I was on assignment."

"Bobby wanted you killed."

Michael raised an eyebrow. "Beau and Dave?"

Jaxson nodded.

"Figures. I always felt those two were keeping tabs on me."

"And yet, all these years later, you've stayed in touch with the entire Crazy Eights group. It would seem the assignment became more than just a job for you."

"They were a good group, most of them," Michael said. "Even Beau and Dave. I knew Bobby was threatening them. And we were much younger then. Ultimately, the friendship kept me in the group long after Bobby was gone."

"And love?"

A slight smile slipped across Michael's lips. "Is it that evident?"

"It's hard to hide adoration. Trust me, I know. When did you and Tú begin dating?"

"Right after Bobby died. She was married to Bobby briefly, though they didn't make it obvious."

Tú was the woman who had told Judith she was Bobby's wife. Jaxson wondered if Holiday knew. Was Judith still up when Tú and Holiday returned to the Grand Mansion Suite to wipe it down? Jaxson tried to piece together the timeline in his head.

"She said he was her biggest mistake." Michael smiled. "She says I am her biggest surprise. I tell her she's mine. You're right. We are very much in love."

"Why not share the same room? Why all the secrecy?"

Michael shrugged. "Ask her. I'm ready for more, but she's not. Until then, I won't push. I'll do anything for her. I'll wait forever for her if I have to."

"The definition of love." Jaxson stood. "Oh, one more thing. Did you and Daily get along well in recent years?"

"Oh, yeah, we kept in touch. In fact, I was going to lease a gallery from her in Rock Hill."

"I didn't know you were interested in art. What about your work as a chef? Were you dropping that?"

He shook his head. "I just wanted to be more diversified. I'm a businessman, first and foremost. If there is something I think I can sell, I will. I suggested Rock Hill and found the place. She bought it, and I leased it from her. We were going to set it up there next month."

"What happens now that Daily is gone? Do you get to keep the gallery?"

"No, but I'm not worried about that. Daily herself is a much bigger loss. I'm unsure how we will ever get over it." He suddenly seemed to remember that Holiday was missing and placed a hand on Jaxson's shoulder. "But, hey, man, don't worry about Holiday. We're gonna find her. I promise."

Jaxson nodded and swallowed hard. "I needed to hear

that. And I needed someone to trust. I don't know what I would do if..."

The back door of the sunroom slammed open.

"We found something, Jax," Christopher said. "Hurry!"

They raced down the back steps three at a time and sprinted across the back lawn.

H oliday pulled the blanket tighter around her body as she stared at Daily's name written on the wall.

This is where Daily had been before she'd been found at the bottom of the stairs. She would never walk back up those stairs. She would never sit where Holiday was seated. She would never write her name again.

Had Daily hidden in this space voluntarily when she didn't show for dinner, or was she taken against her will? Maybe the killer had hidden her until he knew what to do. Or perhaps he hadn't known about this place at all. Maybe Daily had used it to stay out of sight and later met her killer and her death at the top of the spiral staircase.

It didn't matter now.

Daily, her childhood best friend, who'd never stopped loving her and kept watch over her despite Holiday's betrayal, was gone.

"I'll never get to say I'm sorry. Or tell you again how much I love you. Or see your pretty face and beautiful smile, or hear your wonderful laugh."

Tears fell from Holiday's eyes.

Daily would never paint another canvas. She'd never welcome another customer into her gallery. She would never find another missing work of art. The artist who'd done so much for Charleston would never be able to contribute again to the city she called home.

And yet, Daily seemed to be everywhere. In the mirror of her bathroom. On the plank in this darkened room. On the bracelet inside the desk.

There was something else beneath her name. Holiday struggled to make it out.

And then she knew. It was that same backward checkmark. Daily had written it twice. Why? What did it mean?

The rustling of keys outside the room interrupted her thoughts. The door crept open, and she saw the silhouette of the man who'd hidden her. He lifted his finger to his lips.

"I'll be back," he whispered. "Shh."

He closed the door and locked it, and Holiday counted each of his fading footsteps until she could hear them no more.

Beau, Dave, Payton, and Tú stood in a circle near the back parking lot. Dave had a flashlight trained on the ground. As Jaxson, Christopher, and Michael drew near, Jaxson spotted one of Holiday's sandals.

"She was here," said Tú.

"Did anyone hear a car pull out?" Michael asked. "Or a van or truck?"

"I don't think we could have," Tú said. "Not from inside the mansion."

Christopher raised his hand a little. "I was outside, looking for Holiday, after I didn't find her in your room. But I didn't hear anything."

"But you looked around the house for her first," Tú said. "I saw you running around."

"Michael, Tú, and I were in the library talking about the night Bobby—" Beau said.

"Oh, my God, don't say it." Payton crossed her arms. "Why is everyone here dying? First Bobby. Then Daily. Then Holiday."

Jaxson took a step toward Payton. "Is she? Is Holiday dead, Payton? How do you know this?"

"What? No! I mean, I was just—"

Dave took a step toward Jaxson. "Don't attack my wife. She had nothing to do with any of this."

"Jaxson's got a point," Tú said. "Why would you say that Holiday's dead, Payton, if there was a chance she's still alive? Maybe you know something we don't?"

Dave pointed an angry finger at Tú. "You stay out of this. How do we know you didn't kill everyone?"

Michael stepped between Dave and Tú. "If you want to talk to her, you talk to me."

Dave scoffed. "You don't know how lucky you are. Maybe Bobby was right about you."

"What's that supposed to mean?" Michael asked.

"Look at us," Christopher said. "Do you see what is happening? Holiday is missing, and the killer now has us at each other's throats. Instead of fighting him, we are fighting each other. Holiday needs our help. Now is not the time for arguing."

"He's right," Jaxson said. He picked up Holiday's shoe and studied it. "She left this on purpose. She wanted to tell us where she was last on the property."

"Or maybe the killer wanted us to think she's gone so we wouldn't look for her," Beau said. "Maybe he planted the shoe next to the car lot."

"Which would mean she's still on the property," Dave said.

"That would be great news," Tú said, "but it's a long shot."

Jaxson's phone buzzed with an incoming message. "He says we are to go back inside and wait for his instructions."

"Oh, my God, he's watching us," Payton said.

Jaxson motioned toward the house. "Come on."

They trekked across the back lawn and agreed to wait in the parlor.

Payton ran up alongside Jaxson. "Listen, I'm sorry back there. I didn't mean...I thought she was already...I'm just scared. I want to get out of here."

Jaxson forced a smile. "I understand." He leaned in closer to Payton. "Did Bobby ever tell Dave why he wanted to go out to Fort Sumter the day he was killed? Holiday said that Bobby kept looking for something when they went there. Could it have been drugs?"

"It was a sack full of money," Payton whispered. "Hundreds of thousands of dollars. Dave said Bobby needed cash to expand his distributions into Charleston. He'd found someone willing to lend him the money. The drop point was Fort Sumter, of all places."

"Whatever happened to the money after Bobby died?" Jaxson asked. "Was it stolen?"

"That's a good question. We never reported it to the police because that would have meant disclosing Dave's involvement. But Dave said that when Bobby returned that day, he saw the paper sack under Bobby's arm. Dave asked him if he had a safe in his room, but Bobby laughed and said he had a better hiding place for the money than a hotel safe. And that was all that was said."

Everyone filed up the steps, through the sunroom, and into the parlor. Some sat. Some stood.

And Jaxson checked his watch.

How long she'd been in the room, Holiday didn't know. The man had taken her phone. Said it was best this way. The darkness, solitude, and the inability to mark time filled her with dread. She wanted to see Jaxson. She wanted to know what was going to happen. And she didn't want the man to come back.

He had said the hardest part would be at the end.

Her mind drifted back to Daily.

Daily had never been one to do things without purpose. Even when she'd disappeared the night before, she'd left messages she knew only Holiday would find. Like the mirror. And maybe like the message in this little room. Did she know Holiday would find this one as well?

Holiday imagined that night again, twenty years ago. Daily snuck into the Grand Mansion Suite through the unlocked door, fearful that Holiday might be in there and that Bobby had hurt her. Bobby was dead on his bed. Holiday was knocked out on one of the chairs.

Then, Daily was standing in the parlor watching Mrs. Rainier sleep. In a moment, Daily hit upon a plan to save her best friend from being accused of murder and resolved to discover who'd killed Bobby Boudreaux. She must've known the plan wouldn't be realized immediately. It would take time. Years. Eventually, the plan took decades.

But that was Daily. Never one to give up. Never one to shirk from what she saw as her duty. She'd even moved to Charleston to be near the crime scene. She painted. She sold her art. And she investigated. And, when she'd assembled the case, she'd called them all to join her at the mansion one last time.

It would be the last time. Daily would've known it would

likely be the end of the Crazy Eights. And then, just when she'd gotten everyone together, ready to reveal Bobby's killer, she would disappear. She would drop the clues and make the group, working together, smoke out the killer among them.

Daily must've known that leaning into Bobby's death might threaten her own life. But she'd made a contingency plan for that as well. Just in case she couldn't see the mystery to its end, she left clues that only Holiday would know. The message on the foggy mirror. Her name on the rustic plank. Even Mrs. Rainier, whom she knew would be at the mansion the same weekend, just as she always was.

Holiday heard the keys again. And when the door opened, the man curled his long index finger and beckoned her to follow.

"It's time," he said. "Now we get to the hard part."

I'm so scared.

18

E veryone was in the parlor waiting when they heard the scream. It came from one of the mansion's top floors.

A piercing, blood-curdling scream that snaked its way down the grand staircase.

Holiday's scream.

And then half a dozen deadening thuds.

Jaxson was out of the parlor at once, bounding up the grand staircase, the others on his heels. He didn't stop on the second or third floors. He instinctively knew Holiday's scream and the thumping sounds that'd followed had come from the uppermost floor. He ran past the elevator and down the hall.

At the bottom of the spiral staircase lay Holiday, a pool of blood surrounding her head, her hair splayed across the crimson floor, her body a crumpled, unmoving mass just below the last step.

Jaxson stopped cold, as if afraid to go forward, uncertain how to begin helping his wife or, even worse, doing anything that might make the awful scene before him true.

Christopher knelt beside Holiday, placed his fingers on the side of her neck, and, with his eyes lowered to her lifeless body, shook his head. He took off his oversized yellow coat and laid it over her. The jacket covered her entirely.

Holiday was gone.

Just like Bobby.

Just like Daily.

Jaxson dropped to his knees. "I can't believe it. My Holiday. She's..."

"Oh, my God," Michael said.

"What's going on around here?" Dave asked. "Everyone is..."

Jaxson looked up at the others standing over him, fury in his eyes, a shaking finger pointing at them. "You. One of you did this to my Holiday."

There were anxious glances from one to the other. Glares of accusations. Rebuffs of denial.

"I would never..." Payton started.

"She was my friend," Tú said.

"We will get him, Jax," Beau said.

"We were all with you, Jax," Christopher said. "In the parlor."

Jaxson boosted himself to his feet, and a box of white Tic Tacs fell from the front pocket of his shirt to the floor. Snarling, he threw the candy across the room. The tiny clear box exploded against the wall, scattering the miniature white mints through the air like shrapnel all around the base of the stairs. He placed his head in his hands and slumped to his knees.

"Holiday... Holiday..."

He lifted his head and pointed to the top of the spiral staircase.

"Up there," he whispered so only the group could hear. "The killer. He must be…"

Michael was the first to move. "I'll go. Everyone, stay here."

It made sense for it to be Michael, the former narcotics officer. He took the stairs two at a time. But not like they'd all just taken the grand staircase. That had been a frenzied panic. Michael moved with deliberate stealth, easing himself along, keeping his head up, just as he'd been trained. Was Michael armed? There was no weapon in his hand.

Then he was at the top, out of sight of the group, and Jaxson could hear him pausing and telling them that he would check the observation deck. The door opened, and after a few moments of strangled tension, it opened again, and Michael came back down the spiral staircase.

He shook his head. "There's nobody up there."

"But how could he have gotten away?" Beau asked.

"The elevator," Tú said.

"While we were coming up, he was going down?" Jaxson asked.

"But I didn't hear the elevator," Payton said.

"How does this keep happening?" Beau asked.

"It's like a ghost …" Dave looked around, almost as if he'd been embarrassed to reveal what he feared.

Jaxson stood over his wife. "It's over."

Christopher placed his large hand on Jaxson's shoulder. "Yes, my friend, it is over."

And then Christopher smiled. A wide, toothy, brilliant smile.

Jaxson knelt before Holiday's body and slowly removed Christopher's large coat.

He placed a gentle hand on the top of Holiday's bloody head. "It's time, my love."

Holiday opened her eyes, and that familiar smile Jaxson loved so much spread across her face.

"Oh, my God!" Payton said.

"What's going on?" Dave asked.

"It's over," Jaxson said again to his wife, smoothing the matted hair from her face. "You can get up now."

"How did I do, dear?" she asked.

"Beautiful as always." Jaxson looked up at the startled onlookers. "Welcome to the Bridgewater version of a murder mystery theater. If you will all be so kind as to follow Christopher downstairs to the parlor, we will begin Act Two."

"What is the meaning of this?" Beau demanded.

"Don't you know?" Jaxson asked.

Beau shook his head, and Jaxson looked at each of the confused faces staring at him.

"I'm going to do exactly as you charged me." He helped Holiday to her feet. "I'm going to reveal your murderer."

It took a good half-hour to get everyone seated in the parlor. Leonard had brought in a few folding chairs, but Michael and Beau, with the help of Beau's crutches, remained standing near the grandfather clock.

Jaxson leaned against the beautiful Italian marble fireplace and touched the mantle. The marble was smooth and cool.

"This better be good." Beau's tone was tart. "That little stunt you two pulled wasn't cool."

"I agree," Payton said. "I'll probably have to see a therapist after this."

Jaxson raised a brow at Holiday, who sighed and smiled. Her hair was a tangled, bloody rat's nest, and she'd donned Jaxson's fedora to cover it.

She has never been more adorable.

Christopher sat in the wide doorway across from the elevator and the grand staircase. Next to him was the man in a blue coat and tie. Jaxson didn't know his name, only that he was a friend of Christopher's. Detective Bonetti stepped into the doorway to Jaxson's left. And two police officers stood guard at the door to the sunroom on his right. Every entrance to the room was completely blocked.

"Who are all these people?" Michael demanded. "And what are the cops doing here?"

Jaxson shrugged. "You said you wanted me to find the murderer among you. What were we going to do with our murderer once we had him...or her?"

Michael shuffled slightly, nodded, and dropped his eyes to the floor.

"But Michael's right. I do need to introduce a few newcomers to you. The officers to my right... I don't know who they are, but I'm pretty sure they came with Detective Bonetti to my left. You may have seen the detective here last night.

"I agree with these folks, Bridgewater," Bonetti said. "This better be good. I left my wife in bed for this, and she was none too happy about it either."

"Thank you, Detective," Holiday said. "Tell your sweet wife it was wonderful that she loaned you to us for just a bit."

The detective smacked his lips and huffed a little but seemed pleased enough with Holiday's acknowledgments.

Beau cut his eyes to Jaxson. "Why did we spend several hours looking for a woman who not only wasn't in danger but was actually hiding from us? I have a good mind to call my lawyer about this."

Jaxson placed his hands together. "Would you be so kind as to introduce your visitor, Christopher?"

Christopher raised his hulking frame from the chair and motioned to the man beside him. "This is my friend, Juan Sanchez, one of the teachers at my school. He teaches theater arts. He's also an accomplished actor, and today, he played the role of Detective Wright of the Charleston Police Department."

"Impersonating a police officer?" Michael nodded to Bonetti. "Kinda sketchy, isn't it, Detective?"

Bonetti grunted again and twirled his finger as if to say, *Keep it rolling.*

"Juan's role was to whisk Holiday to a secure location here at the mansion," said Jaxson, "the purpose of which was to smoke out our murderer."

"Did she know?"

Jaxson turned to Payton. "Yes, she knew the charades we would play tonight. Five of us knew."

Tú ticked off the names on her fingers. "You, Holiday, Christopher, and Juan." She looked around the room. "Who was the fifth?"

"That would be me." Leonard gave her a pleasant smile. "I don't mind saying I've had a generous amount of thespian experience in my life, and it was quite fun playing the minor role of deceiver."

"It was Leonard who unwittingly gave me the idea of creating this game of charades," Jaxson said. "He said something that Holiday and I might use in our next novel. He said that if you want to catch a killer, you must think not like the murderer but like the victim."

"I must clarify," Leonard added quickly. "Those are not my words but Miss Southerleigh's. It's what she told me she was doing to catch Mr. Boudreaux's murderer."

"And it's what Holiday and I decided to do to catch Daily's killer," Jaxson said. "In Daily's own words, we would replay the day by thinking like the victim." He glanced at Holiday. "Like Daily."

"Okay, I'm confused and bored, and I'm not staying for any more of this utter nonsense." Dave looked at his wife. "Come on, Payton, we're checking out."

"No, you're not!" Bonetti's voice boomed across the parlor, and he pointed a thick finger at Dave. "No one leaves this room until I say you leave this room."

Dave nodded, the detective twirled his finger again, and Jaxson continued.

"As everyone knows, Bobby Boudreaux was a dealer. Heroin. Meth. Ecstasy. Crack. He was a one-stop shop. He sold on campus and off while he and the other seven members of the Crazy Eights were college students, and he continued to do so after graduation. He also hired two group members to join him in his enterprise: Dave and Beau. The last and final member of the Crazy Eights also began selling for Bobby, but that final member was working undercover as a narcotics agent. He wasn't so much trying to get Bobby off the streets as he was trying to get to his source." Jaxson turned to Michael. "Do I have that right?"

Michael nodded. "Perfect."

"So, you really were a cop?" Beau shook his head in disbelief. "I thought Bobby was just being paranoid."

"I think it might be fair to say that Bobby was a user,"

Jaxson said. "I'm not speaking about drugs. I'm talking about people. Holiday, could I have our first exhibit?"

Holiday handed him the deck of playing cards she'd found in the library. "Bobby found these cards twenty years ago and marked them with your names. Each of you was to play a role in his plans."

He held up the eight of hearts. "Three names. First Tú, crossed out. Then Daily. It, too, was crossed out. And finally, Holiday, also crossed out. Each of you was to be, for Bobby, his love interest. But in turn, the three of you dumped him, and when that happened, he moved on."

"Who became his love interest after Holiday?" asked Michael.

"I'm gonna get to that." Jaxson held up the eight of diamonds. "Tú's and Holiday's names were written here before they were crossed out. If the hearts represent love, the diamonds represent money for his drug enterprise."

"He's right," said Dave. "Bobby thought Tú would fund his business. Then he wanted Holiday's money. But then he found another source."

"Who was the other source?" Holiday asked.

Dave shook his head. "We never did know."

"Whoever it was," Jaxson said, "they left a paper sack full of money at Fort Sumter, and Bobby picked it up and took it back to the inn the day he died." He held up the eight of clubs. "Bobby's henchmen. Dave and Beau. Sorry for the ugly title, but that's what you were to Bobby. You were to do his dirty work. He even wanted you to kill Michael the night Bobby was killed."

Michael cut flaming eyes toward them.

"We weren't going to do it," Dave said.

"Bobby had us, Michael. You know that," Beau said. "Dave's right. We weren't going to do it, but—"

"And the eight of spades," Jaxson held it high for all to see. "Michael. A spade with which you might dig your own grave, perhaps?" Jaxson put the card away and pulled out four others. "Bobby had written himself on all the kings. He wanted it all. But there was one more person to play a role."

"Me," Payton said.

Everyone turned toward her.

"You were to be his queen of hearts, isn't that right, Payton? The two of you were having an affair."

Dave spun toward his wife. "Is this true? You and Bobby? While we were married?"

"You were the collateral, Payton," Jaxson said. "If Dave didn't continue to sell, Bobby would've ratted you out to Dave, and your marriage would've been destroyed."

"That's why you never stopped me," Dave said. "I always thought it curious that my own wife never once told me to stop selling."

"Don't blame me," Payton snapped. "You're the one who wanted to sell. I questioned you before you started, and you did it anyway."

Jaxson handed the cards to Bonetti, who rifled through them. "Each of you had a motive, a reason to kill Bobby. Beau and Dave needed a way out. Payton needed her relationship with Bobby to go to the grave with him. Michael, you figured Bobby had marked you as a dead man. And Tú..." Jaxson walked back to the fireplace. "This one really stumped me. I couldn't determine if you even had a motive until you said something during your spa appointment. Do you remember what you said?"

Tú shook her head slightly.

"You said that a man will only succeed to the degree that the most powerful woman in his life will allow. Do you remember that?"

Tú swallowed. "I remember."

"You were in charge of Bobby. You were his boss, in love, and in work. Am I right?"

Tú licked her lips. "What do you want me to say, Jax?"

"You were Bobby's supplier. The drug business is what got the two of you together. With his contacts, his money, and the drugs you could get your hands on, you saw your-self as a power couple. The only thing was, Bobby didn't have the money he told you he did."

"Bobby was a liar, in many ways, to many people."

"A liar and a thief, yes, but something else he did really angered you. That was when he decided to expand the busi-ness without you, and in your own backyard. I'm guessing the idea of selling here in Charleston didn't originate with him but from someone who'd grown up in South Carolina. He stole your idea and found someone else with the cash to implement the plan."

Tú stared at him, her eyelids flickering.

"I'm simply establishing motive," Jaxson said. "You see, I must do that with the mysteries I write. I must explain to the reader why a particular character would want to kill a victim. In real life, a jury doesn't need a motive to convict, though it helps. But in the world of fiction, if there's no motive, there's no credibility. And believe me when I say that you, Miss Dinh, had plenty of motive."

Jaxson turned back to the group. "You all did, except for one person. And she was the one you all decided would be the fall guy. Perhaps I should say fall gal? The trip to Wentworth Mansion was a business trip to expand Bobby's empire. But there was one other purpose, and that involved the killing of Michael. The night Bobby was killed, Beau and Dave would bring Michael to Bobby's room and kill him. Everything would be staged to make it look like Holiday had done it. She was the wild card."

Jaxson slipped the joker playing card from his pocket and turned it around so the group could see Holiday's name. Then he handed it to Bonetti.

"The problem was, one of you killed Bobby before Michael could be killed, someone who didn't know the plan. Someone in this room right now."

19

———————

The members of the Crazy Eights craned their heads around the room toward each other as if to say, "Was it you?" But Jaxson noted that two Crazy Eights, while they turned around, did not look at each other, and he smiled. He was on the right track.

Dimly lit and crowded, the parlor was deathly quiet, aside from Detective Bonetti, arms crossed, tapping his foot.

"Dave and I knew the plan," Beau said. "We didn't kill Bobby."

"You could've," Jaxson said. "Just because you knew the plan doesn't mean you didn't do it. The two of you could've killed him. You may have even discussed it among yourselves. But no, you didn't murder Bobby. It was someone else in this room who didn't know that Michael was to be killed that night."

"That would leave Tú, Payton, and of course Michael," Christopher called from the back of the room.

"You're right. But only one of them left something behind in Bobby's room." Jaxson paced past Payton, Michael, and Tú.

Then he stood in front of Tú.

"If only you hadn't dropped that bracelet."

Tú offered the room a bewildered smile. "You can't be serious. You can't possibly...What bracelet are you even talking about?"

Jaxson turned to Holiday. "Exhibit B, dear."

Holiday held up her ankle so everyone could see the gold triple-strand rope bracelet with Daily's name.

"That says Daily," Tú said. "That's not mine."

Holiday unfastened the bracelet and held it out.

"You see this?" Jaxson asked. "The clasp and the charms are made of a newer metal than the rest. They were added later. Daily did that. Daily found the bracelet, modified it so it wouldn't fall off, as it did for you, and added her initials to disguise it until she used it as evidence."

Jaxson thumbed up the photo of the Crazy Eights standing at the top of Reunion Tower and held the phone for all to see. "I got this photo from you, Tú. You shouldn't have let me send it to myself. The photo and losing the bracelet when you entered Bobby's room was your undoing." He held the phone close to Tú. "You see, you have on the same bracelet, except without the charms. It's yours, alright, and you dropped it in Bobby's room the night you went in there to murder him."

"I could've dropped that bracelet anywhere," Tú said. "Plus, even if Daily did find it, she's not here now to tell you it was mine."

"Actually, she can," Jaxson said. "She told us yesterday before she was killed. Holiday, do you have the photo of the foggy mirror with the message Daily left for you?"

Holiday thumbed open the last photo and held it up for others to see.

"This is one of the ways Daily and Holiday would send

secret messages to each other. Before she was killed, she must've known her life could be in danger. So, just in case, she passed along a clue to Holiday. It was a left-handed checkmark."

"I don't think Daily was left-handed," Payton said.

"Neither do I," Jaxson said, "which means this is not a checkmark." He pointed to the old grandfather clock. "Holiday, would you go draw the lefthanded checkmark on the clock face starting with the number twelve?"

Holiday stood in front of the old clock and, with one finger, drew an imaginary line down to the center of the dial and then back up, just like the backward checkmark. When her finger touched the number two, she gasped and turned toward the group.

"Two...for Tú," she said. "This is what she wanted us to discover. You killed Bobby."

"You are out of your mind!" Tú exclaimed. She turned to the faces staring at her. "You know they're both crazy, right? This doesn't prove I killed Bobby. Plus, I wasn't even here when Bobby died. I was at my grandmother's when Holiday called me."

"That's a lie, and I can prove it," said Jaxson.

He turned to Leonard, sitting between Christopher and the old grandfather clock. "Would you be so kind as to go and get exhibit C, if I may call her that?"

Leonard smiled and exited the parlor, returning within a few seconds and escorting Judith Rainier to a seat.

"Is it my turn now?" Mrs. Rainier asked. She turned to Holiday. "There's my friend."

Holiday smiled at her.

Jaxson pointed to Tú. "Mrs. Rainier, on the night that Bobby Boudreaux died, did you see this woman?"

Mrs. Rainier nodded. "Yes. I have a perfect memory for

faces. She told me she was Mr. Boudreaux's wife and wanted to know which room he was in."

Jaxson turned back to Tú. "Here's what I believe happened. You got here and ran into sweet Mrs. Rainer in the sunroom next door. You went into the lobby, right outside the Grand Mansion Suite, and pulled a bottle and a couple of glasses out of a big bag Mrs. Rainer saw over your shoulder. Maybe you knocked and then hid. Or maybe you waited upstairs or outside. It doesn't matter because Bobby took the bait."

"None of this is true," Tú said under her breath.

Jaxson went on. "Did you use a hypodermic needle to inject the midazolam through the cork directly into the wine? I don't know, but somehow you did. Then you waited. And when you figured enough time had gone by, you entered through the door, helped a drunk and passed-out Bobby to his bed, and injected him with the drugs that would kill him. Then you fled. But on your way back to Rock Hill, Holiday called you, and you told her you were at your grandmother's. But of course, you weren't. You weren't even halfway there by then. It took you less than an hour to return to the mansion."

Jaxson turned to Christopher. "My friend, tell the group how long a drive it is from Rock Hill to Charleston."

"At a minimum, depending on traffic, I would say a good two and a half, maybe three hours."

Jaxson spun back to Tú. "There's no way you were at your grandmother's when Holiday called. But let me ask you something. Is that when you realized your bracelet was missing? Because, you see, I don't think you would've gone back to rescue Holiday if it hadn't been for that bracelet. You returned because the bracelet had fallen off, and you knew you had to get it out of that room. So, you told Holiday to stay in Room 19 until you arrived, and that's what she did. You didn't come back to help her. You came back to find the evidence you dropped. It must've been a shocker when you discovered that not only was the bracelet gone, but so was the needle you used to inject the lethal dose into a comatose Bobby. Both were gone because Daily came in between your first and second entries into Bobby's room, scooped up both items, and left."

"I'm not saying anything," Tú said.

"That's probably a wise choice," Jaxson said. "Judith, when you saw Daily Southerleigh here in the parlor that night, she asked you to keep a key for her. Is that right?"

Judith held out the chain with the small skeleton key she wore around her neck. "Yes, dear, that is correct. I keep it on this necklace and have for twenty years now."

"Would you give that key to Leonard? I believe it belongs to him."

Mrs. Rainier lifted the necklace over her head and handed it to the innkeeper, who stood by the clock.

"Leonard, have you ever opened that clock?" Jaxson asked.

"Never. There was no key."

Jaxson nodded at the key in the innkeeper's hand. "I believe you have it now."

Leonard slipped the key into the lock on the glass door of the old grandfather clock and turned it smoothly to the left. The door swung open with ease.

"Some of you may be thinking that there's no physical proof Daily was here the night Bobby died," Jaxson said. "There is. Her name is written in the old registry in the lobby by the front door. She checked in just after Holiday. We suspect she was here to keep an eye on Holiday, knowing that her best friend had come to the inn with a drug dealer. Sometime after Bobby was killed, Daily entered his room. She saw him dead on the bed, and her best friend passed out in a chair. She had to think of something fast. And that's when she saw your bracelet, which told her you had been in that room. And she also found something else. Leonard, would you look inside the clock's casing? And be careful when you do."

Leonard reached inside the clock and gingerly removed an old hypodermic needle.

"And now I give you Exhibit D," Jaxson said. "Just where it's been for the last twenty years."

"A time capsule of murder," Christopher said.

"Stop!" Bonetti bellowed. "That's evidence you're touching. Officer, bag that before it gets contaminated further."

Jaxson nodded. "He's right. I believe DNA analysis will demonstrate that this is the needle that was used to kill Bobby. And it's probably got your DNA on it, also, Tú. You left it and your bracelet when you left his room that night."

"Is this true, young lady?" Bonetti asked. "Did you kill that young man twenty years ago?"

Tú crossed her legs and looked down at her hands folded neatly in her lap. "I want a lawyer."

Bonetti gave a hearty, sardonic laugh. "I bet you do. Officer Tulmy, cuff this young woman and take her to the other room. Read her rights to her, and put her in your car."

Tú stood as the officer approached, her arms stretched before her, wrists together. She looked at Holiday as the cuffs were fastened. "Bobby was always the smartest guy in the room, according to him. But he made two mistakes. First, he underestimated me. And second, he underestimated you, too, Holiday Trousseau."

"Bridgewater," Holiday said. "Holiday Bridgewater."

Tú smirked and winked at Jaxson. "You remember what I said, Jax."

The officer paraded Tú from the room, reading her Miranda rights as they went.

"So, Tú killed Bobby, and then she killed Daily to cover it up?" Dave asked.

"Almost," Jaxson said. "Somebody else killed Daily. Christopher, what did you find at the top of the spiral staircase after we were all downstairs?"

"Nothing, my good friend."

"You didn't find a box of yellow Sprite Tic Tacs?"

"I found nothing up there."

Jaxson turned to Michael. "That's because you have it, don't you?"

Michael cut his eyes around the room.

Jaxson pulled a small, clear bag from his pocket. "I need you to pull it out of your pocket and drop it in this bag."

"You're kidding, right?" Michael reached into his front pants pocket, pulled out the small Tic Tac container, and dropped it in the baggie. "Yeah, I had a box of mints, but I didn't find them on the stairs leading to the cupola. I found them in the yard today, and you can't prove otherwise."

"Actually, I can prove it," Jaxson said. "You see, just before tonight's little game began, I wiped down this little box before Holiday pretended to fall down the spiral staircase. It doesn't have my fingerprints on it anymore. I gave it to Juan, and he's the one who placed it on the floor of the cupola." Jaxson walked over to Bonetti and handed him the transparent bag. "When the police dust it for prints, they're only going to find two sets: Juan's and yours."

The color drained from Michael's face, and he dropped into the empty chair beside him.

"Yesterday, I dropped a candy box, and Michael picked it

up. He hadn't thought much about it until he saw mints fall from my pocket tonight. And that's when he wondered whether he'd dropped my box of Tic Tacs up there when he pushed Daily down the stairs. Suddenly, Michael, you had a chance to look. I needed someone to see if our murderer was up there, and you straight-up volunteered."

Michael closed his eyes.

"When you went upstairs to see who had supposedly killed Holiday, you saw this box and pocketed it. I can only imagine what you must've thought about your good fortune to find the evidence that you'd been up there when Daily was pushed down."

Michael's eyes were open again, but they were sad eyes now, distant and staring.

"There's only one reason why someone would take the time to pocket a little box of yellow Tic Tacs when he's supposedly looking for a killer who's just pushed a woman to her death down a spiral staircase, and that's because he was hiding evidence that would convict him of murder." Jaxson let out a long breath. "I'm gonna be honest with you, Michael. I suspected it was you, but I wasn't sure until you picked up that box of Tic Tacs."

Michael swore under his breath, and Jaxson turned to the group.

"Michael and Tú have had a relationship for twenty years. He loves her as much as any man could love a woman, so much so that he was willing to kill to cover up a murder Tú committed two decades earlier. And Daily was also a threat to their growing drug business."

Jaxson turned to Michael. "That's what the conversation I overheard from the top of the spiral staircase was about yesterday. Am I right? You and Tú had too much at stake, professionally and personally, to allow Daily to bring forth the evidence to convict Tú."

"But you ran up to the cupola after Daily fell and looked for someone, right?" Payton asked. "You said nobody was up there."

"I did," Jaxson said. "Michael, all you had to do was open the trap door on the walkway up there and slip beneath the deck. And there you waited while the authorities came. And when their investigation was complete, and we were all downstairs, you slipped back into your room."

Holiday raised her hand as though they were in school, which made Jaxson smile. "But what about the needle we found in the armoire in our room, which I supposedly hid?"

"Planted by Michael," Jaxson said. "At some point, he hid it in the baseboard of the armoire and then told us the story about you with a needle in your hand. The whole idea was to make it look as though you had killed Bobby, and we would all just assume you'd killed Daily as well."

Jaxson turned to Michael.

"You and Tú tried to frame my wife for murder, with the needle and message on the mirror. You wanted me to doubt her innocence and back off the case. But do you want to know something? I never doubted Holiday's innocence. She was never a suspect. She was always my Watson."

"You put the slippery stuff at the top of the spiral staircase?" Payton asked Michael.

Michael looked up. "That wasn't me. I don't even know what that was."

"He's right," Jaxson said. "He didn't make the floor up there slimy. Beau did."

Every eye turned to Beau.

"What? That's crazy." Beau pointed to his walking boot

on his leg. "Why would I deliberately almost kill myself on those stairs?"

Jaxson turned to Leonard again. "May I have Exhibit E, our next witness?"

Leonard left the room and returned with an elderly man about the same age as Mrs. Rainer. He wore a brown suit with a red tie and walked with a slight stoop. He sat in one of the empty chairs next to Mrs. Rainier.

"Are you Dr. Miller?" Jaxson asked.

"I am."

"Would you tell us about your diagnosis for our friend Beau over there with the crutches? I believe you examined him last night after his fall down the stairs."

The doctor shook his head. "I can't do that. I didn't get to examine him. He told me his leg wasn't hurt when I got to his room. He said his friends were insistent that he be examined. He paid me for the visit, and I left just as instructed."

"You didn't prescribe Beau the crutches and a walking boot?"

"Nope. Didn't bring them with me, and as far as I know, he doesn't need them."

"Thank you, doctor, that will be all. You are free to go if you like."

The doctor looked around the room. "I'll stay if it's all the same to you."

Jaxson turned to Beau.

"Your foot isn't hurt. You didn't fall down the spiral staircase. You poured the slippery stuff on the floor of the cupola, then staged your fall so that you could get out of the room you were in, the one Daily chose for you, and into the Grand Mansion Suite on the main floor."

"Why would you want to be back in the same room where Bobby was murdered?" Payton asked.

Beau didn't answer, so Jaxson did. "For the money. When Bobby returned from a visit to Fort Sumter, he had a bag of cash with him—hundreds of thousands of dollars. And Bobby thought he was too smart to lock the money up in the safe in his room. Maybe he thought the inn's staff would steal it from him. So, he told Dave and Beau he had a better place for it."

Bonetti spoke up. "Are you saying there is a sack with hundreds of thousands of dollars hidden in this beautiful old mansion right now?" The detective turned to Leonard. "When word gets out, you'll be inundated with treasure seekers. People won't be able to get a room here for years."

Leonard put praying hands together. "Let's just hope they're not killers."

"Mr. Leonard," Mrs. Rainier said in her precise, small voice, "don't forget to save my room for me every October. I don't want treasure hunters stealing mine and Arthur's room."

Leonard promised her the room was secure, then he turned to Beau. "So, you're not hurt? Did you find the money?"

Beau shook his head. "I have turned that room upside down looking for it. It's not there. Either someone else found it or, as Jaxson said, it's hidden somewhere else in this house."

"You reserved the Grand Mansion Suite under a fake name, I would guess, then canceled it an hour before you staged your accident, making it available for you to acquire," Jaxson said.

"Why not just request that room from the beginning?" Payton asked.

"Daily reserved the rooms," Jaxson said. "Remember?

She put most of you in the same rooms you were all in the night Bobby died."

"Did you really bring your crutches and walking boot?" Holiday asked.

Beau gave them a sheepish grin.

"I was wondering when I moved your suitcase to the Grand Mansion Suite yesterday," said Jaxson, "what you could possibly need that was so heavy for one short weekend. By the way, don't run up the stairs the next time you pretend you need crutches. You came up the stairs just as fast as the rest of us tonight when we heard Holiday scream."

Beau's eyes widened at his goof.

"Oh, one more thing," Jaxson said. "What was that slippery stuff up there? You're lucky I didn't go over the railing yesterday when I got into it. We could've easily had another murder here at Wentworth."

"I'm sorry. It was a dumb plan." Beau rolled his eyes. "It's just castor oil. I only meant for it to be a prop. I never dreamed someone would slip in it."

Detective Bonetti pulled out a set of cuffs and had Michael stand and extend his wrists. "Come on. Let's Mirandize you as well." He led him toward the large door across from the elevator, but turned back to Jaxson. "Well done, young man. I'm gonna want your full story before you leave Charleston. Stay close to the mansion until I get back to you."

Jaxson nodded, and Michael was led away.

Everyone stood and began talking all at once. Holiday pulled Jaxson into the sunroom.

"They knew," she said. "Several of them knew I was going to be here that night. They knew I was Bobby's wildcard. And yet none of them stopped him—my so-called friends. The only reason I didn't get set up for Michael's murder was because Tú killed Bobby first. In a way, she saved my life."

"She put your life in danger, baby. She knew Bobby, and yet she fed you to him." He slipped an arm around her shoulders. "And the only reason she came back was to find her bracelet. If she hadn't lost that bracelet…"

"I love you." She stood on her tiptoes and kissed him. "And you were amazing. You solved Bobby and Daily's murder."

Jaxson pulled her closer and rested his chin on her head. "We solved it together. We make a good crime-fighting team. But truly, you were the amazing one. I couldn't have played dead for as long as you did. I didn't even see you breathing!" He took her face in both of his hands and kissed her again. "By the way, where were you hiding all that time?"

"Up on the roof. There's a little utility room up there. It was cold and dark. I want to go back up there and see it more clearly when the sun is up."

Jaxson looked at his phone. "Well, that won't be long now."

They sank into the white wicker chairs and got quiet. Jaxson suddenly realized how tired he was from the last twenty-four hours. If he were to close his eyes…

"She still loved me," Holiday said at last. "Daily. And she came here to protect me."

Holiday cried.

Jaxson held her hand.

And they watched the sun come up behind the mansion.

20

———————

I *didn't want to come back. Now, I don't want to leave.*

Holiday peered over her Circa 1886 menu at the three men dining with her in the mansion's celebrated restaurant. She liked being the center of so much male attention.

"Which tasting menu are you boys choosing tonight?" Holiday asked.

Jaxson slipped on his reading glasses and carefully considered his choices. Christopher and Juan compared the Ashley tasting menu with the Cooper.

"I'm going with the Ashley for no other reason than the southern grilled cheese," Jaxson said.

"Then I'll choose the Cooper, and we can share and try each other's plates," Holiday said.

Christopher and Juan decided to choose both menus.

"They always give you such small portions in fine dining. It'll be like having one regular-size meal," Christopher said.

The hostess came and took their orders, and the four tried their drinks.

Holiday looked around the beautiful restaurant. It was hard to imagine it had once been the mansion's rough carriage house. Freshly cut flowers topped the crisp white tablecloths. The lowering sun filtered through the windows on the two double-wide arched doors that would've allowed the carriages in and out. The horse stalls, now paneled in green hardwood and beautiful white porcelain tile, housed elegant leather booths where diners ate, laughed, and celebrated. Intimate and charming, Circa 1886 was both Southern and sophisticated.

"I like it here, Jax," Holiday said. "Despite everything that happened during this trip—and last—I really like this wonderful, old inn. Can we come back again sometime soon?"

"I would love it. And maybe the next time we do, we won't get stuck searching for a killer."

"How could someone even think of murder in such a beautiful place as Wentworth?"

Jaxson sighed. "All it takes is one little murder to spoil a whole vacation."

Across the room, at a small table, two other guests were dining and oblivious to the celebrating amateur sleuths. Holiday watched Dr. Miller pour a glass of wine and hand it to Mrs. Rainier, who took a sip and nodded for the doctor to fill her glass.

Take a lot of sips from other people's glasses before you decide what to pour into your own.

When he set the bottle down, Mrs. Rainier reached across the table with both hands and held one of his. They both smiled and resumed their dining.

Don't rush, Mrs. Rainier.

"Any updates from the police on the two killers?" Christopher asked.

Jaxson nodded. "I spoke with Bonetti today, and he said Michael is singing like a canary. The love between him and Tú is over."

"Bobby was going to frame me for Michael's murder, and Michael was willing to frame me for Bobby's." Holiday sighed. "And Daily's."

Jaxson took her hand and gave it a little squeeze. "But the truth was on our side."

"I have another question," Christopher said. "Who was Ace?"

"Michael told Bonetti that Tú is Ace. She went by that name in her operation, which she was trying to expand from Charleston to Rock Hill with a second gallery as a front. That's why Michael had signed the agreement with Daily."

"By the way," Holiday said, "Daddy called today."

"Oh?"

"He said he was proud of how you cared for me and solved the mystery," Holiday said.

Jaxson raised his eyebrows. "Anything else?"

Holiday grimaced. "And he asked if this meant you would give up your writing hobby and return to your real job."

Jaxson rolled his eyes. "Sounds like your father."

She reached over and took Jaxson's hand in hers. "I told him you have a real job."

"And that would be...?"

"Writing. And loving me!" She laughed, then leaned into him and whispered. "I'm sorry I didn't tell you about my first visit to Wentworth. I felt so dumb about that weekend and never wanted to think about it again."

Jaxson squeezed her hand. "It's no problem, love. There are many things I don't know about you, but I will spend the rest of my life discovering every wonderful thing about Holiday Trousseau Bridgewater."

"My story is safe with you."

He gave her a curious look.

"That's what Leonard thinks Wentworth Mansion would say if its walls could talk," she said. "Our stories are safe here. And our stories are safe with each other, you and me. We get each other."

"Our stories, secrets, desires, and wishes," Jaxson said. "Everything about you is safe with me." He paused, then added. "And we can return to Wentworth Mansion as often as you like."

"Just like sweet Mrs. Rainier sitting at that table with Dr. Miller." Holiday took a sip of her wine. "Honeymoons. That's what we'll call our trips. Forever on honeymoon."

They continued discussing the weekend, and Holiday remembered her first time at Wentworth Mansion. How different it had been then.

That ceiling looks like our wedding cake.

It was Bobby who'd said that. But that's not exactly what he'd said.

"That ceiling looks like *a* wedding cake."

"What do you mean?" Holiday had asked Bobby.

He'd just come back from Fort Sumter without her that day, twenty years ago. As they sat in the parlor discussing their future, Holiday had told him it would be best if they were just friends, and quite surprisingly, he'd agreed. In his lap was a brown paper sack, and he explained what he meant about the room.

"The plaster designs on the ceiling remind me of the side of my sister's wedding cake," he'd said. "It fits. This room has a lot of layers. You could be looking at one thing and not see something else hidden in plain sight."

Holiday grabbed Jaxson's arm as the memories of Bobby's last day faded in her mind. "Come on! I know where the money is."

She sprinted toward the front door, dragging Jaxson away from the table. Christopher and Juan followed. They ran across the lawn and up the back steps, through the sunroom, and into the parlor. The room was empty and quiet, aside from the inn's light classical music and the warm ticking of the grandfather clock marking time once again in the corner.

"What are we doing here?" Christopher asked.

"You know where the money is, Holiday?" Jaxson asked. "Is it in here?"

Holiday paced the room. "Look around. Someplace where he could've quickly stashed a bag of cash, someplace where nobody would think to look for two decades."

They swept the room. Jaxson opened the grandfather clock. Christopher searched the fireplace. And Juan peeked behind the pictures for a hidden wall safe.

"Here!" Holiday knelt before the inset bookshelf, shining her phone light through the grill at the bottom of the wall. "There's something in there."

Jaxson pulled open a small screwdriver on his pocketknife and got to work on the screws. He pulled the grill away from the wall and set it aside. Holiday shone her phone's light into the darkened crevice as they peered into the hole. Far in the back of the recess was a small, partially flattened, crumpled paper sack.

Christopher reached in and pulled out the sack. He opened it fully and passed it around for the others to see. It was empty, aside from two old ferry tickets to Fort Sumter.

"It's gone," Jaxson said. "Somebody else found the

money but left the bag. That's one mystery we'll never solve."

"I would've been surprised if it had still been here," Christopher said.

"At least sweet Mrs. Rainier won't have to worry about her room," Holiday said, "now that treasure seekers won't flood Wentworth."

No hidden money. No missing evidence. No unsolved murders. Wentworth Mansion had finally yielded all its secrets.

Just like Holiday.

It felt good to be transparent with Jaxson. It felt real and mature. She had Daily to thank for that, too.

Jaxson plopped onto the settee facing the fireplace. "You know, the ceiling does resemble a wedding cake."

Holiday settled down next to him and placed her hand on his. "It looks like our wedding cake, dear."

"Didn't we have the best wedding?" he said. "You were the prettiest thing ever in that dress. No matter where we go, if you're there, I will love it. I will follow you anywhere."

Holiday stood and walked to the parlor's open door. She spun, facing him, hands on her hips. "Well?"

The three men stared at each other.

"Where are you going?" Jaxson asked.

"Back to our room," she said, "and if you follow me there, I'm sure you'll love that too."

Jaxson looked at the other two men, stood, and followed his wife up the grand staircase.

An Heiress Wanted To Die
A Teacher Wanted To Kill
Together They Solved Their Own Murder
How Jaxson Met Holiday!
YOURS FREE! @
THE DRISKILL HOTEL MYSTERY
It only takes one little murder to spoil a whole vacation
PARTNERS in CRIME
RESORTING TO MURDER SERIES
DEREK D. WHEELESS
www.DerekWheelessAuthor.com

AFTERWORD

I've always been fascinated by hotels and inns. Strangers with competing backgrounds and motives coming together under one roof for a night. Dinners shared. Conversations overheard. Secrets behind closed doors. The mysteries the walls could share if they could whisper.

Even more intriguing are the hotels and inns that enjoy a rich, vibrant history and a challenging, complex character. These properties tend to be older, often dating back one hundred years or more, and fabulously luxurious. Often, they've had the most eclectic visitors in their past—movie stars, criminals, athletes, former presidents, and other world leaders. With their luxuriously rich history and heritage, their unique and often unusual architecture, and their own distinct and sometimes complicated personalities and character, it can be an otherworldly experience spending a night or two where mystery, intrigue, and suspense mingle with every guest.

These hotels and inns become characters in their own right.

Oh, and did I mention they all have ghost sightings and

stories? Paranormal activity comes standard with these unconventional and sometimes quite eccentric hotels and inns.

I've been fortunate to visit a few of such wonderfully inviting accommodations. Wentworth Mansion in Charleston. The Grand Hotel on Mackinac Island. Del Coronado in San Diego. The Boca Raton in Boca Raton. The Grand Galvez in Galveston. Grove Park Inn in Asheville. The Driskill in Austin. The Adolphus in Dallas. The Arizona Biltmore in Phoenix. For me, such locations become the perfect setting for a story.

After the publication of my first novel, *We Planned a Murder*, I began to consider the direction I wanted to take next. Would I continue the Nacho Blanco adventures in Ten Spot, Texas, or would I explore a whole different set of characters, conflicts, and mysteries?

I began to consider the possibility of a new series of mysteries, each novel set in a different hotel or inn, featuring a married couple who unwittingly find themselves entangled in a murder investigation wherever they go.

Enter Jaxson and Holiday Bridgewater.

I'm not the first to explore these ideas, at least in part. Author Kathleen Kaska has a historical hotel mystery series set during the mid-1900s. Agatha Christie penned four novels and a book of short stories featuring Tommy and Tuppence, a married couple who found themselves embroiled in one mystery after another. And Dashiell Hammett, who made literary history with the publication of *The Maltese Falcon*, also wrote the equally impressive *The Thin Man*, featuring Nick and Nora Charles, a young couple drinking and dancing their way from one dangerous murder investigation to another during the Jazz Age of the 1930s. The public loved Nick and Nora so much that Hollywood adapted the novel into a movie and subsequently produced four cinematic sequels during the next fifteen years. Nobody could get enough of the fun-loving, high-flying Nick and Nora and their beloved dog Asta.

I set to work mapping out my ideas for this new series, and soon realized that with the writing, there would also be research. In November 2023, I made a trip to Wentworth Mansion, and I knew straightaway, just like Jaxson, that I wanted the first "Resorting to Murder" mystery set at the beautiful, old Gothic home. The parlor (drawing room), the library, the sunroom, the Grand Mansion Suite—it was like entering a real-life game of Clue, minus the weapons and the dead body, of course. Like Jaxson, I immediately went on a photographic scavenger hunt, recording every room that looked like it might help make a good old-fashioned murder mystery. It was only natural that Wentworth Mansion and *Seven For A Secret Never To Be Told* became the first in the "Resorting to Murder" series.

I highly recommend taking a trip to Wentworth Mansion. Play a game of Crazy Eights in the library. Spend the night in the Grand Mansion Suite. Partake of the afternoon hors d'oeuvres in the sunroom. Take the spiral staircase to the top of the cupola and step out on the deck for the most spectacular views of old Charleston. And when the sun goes down, settle into the parlor with a glass of wine and your copy of *Seven For A Secret Never To Be Told*, and imagine Jaxson revealing the murderer as he stands before the beautiful Italian marble fireplace. You'll be right there on the set of the story.

- DDW

Wentworth Mansion.

The Grand Staircase

The Spiral Staircase

The Grand Mansion Suite

The Grand Mansion Suite

The Grand Mansion Suite

The Library

The. Spiral Staircase

The Sunroom

The Parlor

Wentworth At Night

Beautiful Wentworth

The Parlor

Your Secrets Are Safe At Wentworth

Circa 1886

Circa 1886 Bar

Take the mystery
with you
everywhere you go!
THE WENTWORTH MANSION MYSTERY
It only takes one little murder to spoil a whole vacation.
SEVEN
for a
SECRET
never to be
TOLD
RESORTING TO MURDER SERIES
A Jessica & Hakaku Bridgewater Mystery
DEREK D. WHEELESS
www.DerekWheelessAuthor.com

ACKNOWLEDGMENTS

No story is ever written in a vacuum. It takes a village, or at least a good team, to craft a narrative worth writing. I am indebted to several people who helped make *Seven For A Secret Never to Be Told* a reality. First and foremost are my three editors: Barb Goffman, Jimmy Callaway, and Nathan Bransford. They cut and deleted, questioned and provoked, and at times even wanted entire sections rewritten. They contributed to shaping the story into what it became, and I am eternally grateful to them. And since they know Jaxson and Holiday as well as anyone, I hope they will continue to grace me with their wisdom and skills for every volume in the "Resorting to Murder" series.

Second, a huge thank you to Maria Novillo Saravia, who did the beautiful artwork for the cover. Maria worked tirelessly on the cover of *Seven For A Secret Never to Be Told*, providing me with five different concepts initially. I chose one. From that, she gave me three ideas for the next book in the series, *The Eyes of Murder Are Upon You*. And then she gave me several concepts for the prequel, *Partners in Crime*. She wanted to ensure that the books would look amazing when displayed side by side as a series. I couldn't be happier with her work, and I look forward to seeing the covers she creates in the years to come as Jaxson and Holiday continue their travels and investigations.

I also want to take a moment to thank my wonderful beta readers: Jackie Burlingame, Heather "Boo" Petro,

Brooke McCallon, my oldest daughter, Brooke Wheeless, and, of course, my wife, Tiffany. They were the first to read the story, and they provided me with valuable feedback. The story is better because of them.

I also want to thank my writing groups, to which I have belonged for years now. Together, we continually learn more about the art and craft of writing, and you've been with me from the very beginning, encouraging, supporting, suggesting, and critiquing. Fellow writers, you are also my friends. You were there when *We Planned a Murder* was published. And you're here now for the publication of *Seven For A Secret Never To Be Told*. Thank you. I am today because of you.

I would be remiss if I did not offer my sincerest gratitude to the fantastic staff of Wentworth Mansion. Your property is exquisite, your amenities are top-notch, and your service is exemplary. I loved writing a fictional mystery set in Wentworth because I adore the mansion's elegance and charm. You inspired me to write. Thank you!

And finally, I would like to extend my endless gratitude to my wife, Tiffany. You were and continue to be my biggest supporter. Thank you for always believing in me. And thank you for all the fantastic ideas you come up with. Nobody dreams up more ways to kill someone than you. I don't know if I should be impressed or frightened. Probably both!

Thank you very much to all of you. The book you hold in your hands is a testament to each of you.

- DDW

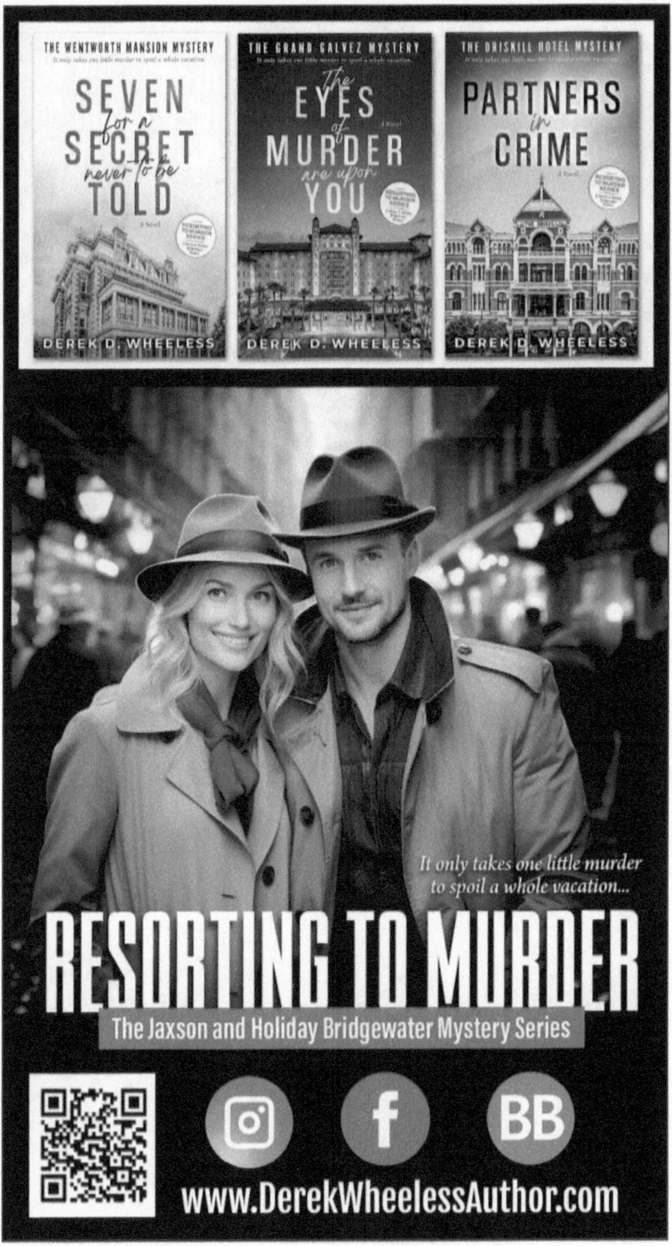
THE WENTWORTH MANSION MYSTERY
SEVEN for a SECRET never to be TOLD
DEREK D. WHEELESS
THE GRAND GALVEZ MYSTERY
The EYES of MURDER are upon YOU
DEREK D. WHEELESS
THE DRISKILL HOTEL MYSTERY
PARTNERS in CRIME
DEREK D. WHEELESS
It only takes one little murder to spoil a whole vacation...
RESORTING TO MURDER
The Jaxson and Holiday Bridgewater Mystery Series
BB
www.DerekWheelessAuthor.com

An Heiress Wanted To Die
A Teacher Wanted To Kill
Together They Solved Their Own Murder
How Jaxson Met Holiday!
YOURS
FREE!
@
THE DRISKILL HOTEL MYSTERY
It only takes one little murder to spoil a whole vacation
PARTNERS in CRIME
DEREK D. WHEELESS
www.DerekWheelessAuthor.com

The Seven Best Friends of Bobby Boudreaux
Six Came Back to Solve His Murder
One Came Back to Kill Again
THE WENTWORTH MANSION MYSTERY
It only takes one little murder to spoil a whole vacation.
SEVEN
for a
SECRET
never to be
TOLD
RESORTING TO MURDER SERIES
DEREK D. WHEELESS
available at
amazon
www.DerekWheelessAuthor.com

If you liked *Seven For A Secret Never To Be Told,* please consider leaving a review on Amazon. Your review might make a difference to another reader who is trying to decide on what to read next, and, with the AI algorithms that Amazon uses, also helps make the novel more visible to potential readers. Thank you!

ABOUT THE AUTHOR

Derek lives in Frisco, Texas, and graduated from Baylor University. He has been a public classroom teacher and school administrator.

Derek has written the short story "Think of the Children" in *Malice in Dallas* as well as "The Prime Witness to the Murder of Dr. Malachi Samson" in *Reckless in Texas*. In addition to *Seven For a Secret Never To Be Told,* he's also written the YA mystery *We Planned a Murder*.